AT THE ROOTS OF THE STARS

D1484264

RJtwaujr
05. 22, 06

Djuna Barnes

AT THE ROOTS
OF THE STARS
The Short Plays

Edited and with an Introduction
by Douglas Messerli

SUN &
MOON

CLASSICS

53

SUN & MOON PRESS
LOS ANGELES • 1995

Sun & Moon Press
A Program of The Contemporary Arts Educational Project, Inc.
a nonprofit corporation
6026 Wilshire Boulevard, Los Angeles, California 90036

This edition first published in paperback in 1995 by Sun & Moon Press
10 9 8 7 6 5 4 3 2 1
FIRST EDITION
©1995 by Sun & Moon Press
Introduction ©1995 by Douglas Messerli
Biographical material ©1995 by Sun & Moon Press
All rights reserved

This book was made possible, in part, through an operational grant from the
Andrew W. Mellon Foundation, through a matching grant from the
National Endowment for the Arts, a nonprofit corporation, and
through contributions to The Contemporary Arts Educational Project, Inc.,
a nonprofit corporation.
Some of these plays were previously published in newspapers and magazines,
*The New York Morning Telegraph Sunday Magazine, Others, Parisienne, Little
Review, Playboy, Vanity Fair, Shadowland,* and *Smart Set,* and in the book
A Night Among The Horses.

Cover: Charles Burchfield, *The Sphinx and the Milky Way*
Munson-Williams-Proctor Institute Museum of Art, Utica, New York
Design: Katie Messborn
Typography: Guy Bennett

LIBRARY OF CONGRESS CATALOGING IN PUBLICATION DATA
Barnes, Djuna [1892–1982]
At the Roots of the Stars: The Short Plays
ISBN: 1-55713-160-0
p. cm — Sun & Moon Classics: 53
American Theater in Literature
I. Title. II. Series.
811'.54—dc20

Printed in the United States of America on acid-free paper.

CONTENTS

Introduction

The plays of Djuna Barnes are unquestionably some of the most curious works of American drama. Combining the realist settings and Irish speech patterns of the plays of J. M. Synge, an Oscar Wildeian sense of wit, and an often sentimental portrait of down-and-out New Yorkers, Barnes's earliest plays are, at best, odd amalgams of styles at war with one another. One must remember that at the time of the earliest plays, *The Death of Life, At the Roots of the Stars*, and *Maggie of the Saints*, Barnes was 25 years old, and she was clearly seeking models. She had read Synge; she published an article on his drama in *New York Morning Telegraph Sunday Magazine* in the weeks between the publication of her first three plays. Family members, on the other hand, purportedly had known Wilde; the family lore was that her great-grandmother had held regular salons which Wilde attended. Mentions of *Salomé*, in particular, show up in Barnes's stories and journalistic writings several times. Accordingly, most of Barnes's early writing for theater, composed at the same time as the fiction she herself described as juvenilia, must be understood as experimentations in which she was working out in dramatic terms the theatrical influences of the day.

Rereadings of her plays, however, reveal far more interesting achievements than this summary allows. Already in *A Passion Play*, published in *Others* in 1918, but certainly by the time of *Three From the Earth* (first performed by the Provincetown Players in 1919) Barnes had begun to use a less realistic and more stylized language and action that would lead her in a direction theatrically closer to her later work. *Three From the Earth*, for example, uses an almost tableau-like setting in which the three Carson brothers, "peasants of the most obvious type," crowded together upon a couch, serve primarily as provocateurs for the worldly Kate Morley as she recounts her affair with their father. Until the final moments of the play, indeed, there is no action: it is all a dialogue of possession, a war of words between the true inheritors of the father's love and the woman who has stolen and squandered that love (she is now engaged to a supreme court judge). When the youngest son—possibly the offspring of Kate and his father's union—steals a photograph and a kiss, the subject of the play is actualized, and the kiss simultaneously becomes a visual emblem of Barnes's theme.

Similarly, in *The Dove*, one of Barnes's most successful plays of this early period, we witness a world not unlike *Hedda Gabler*'s, of two intelligent sisters' intense sexual and imaginative frustration. Like Hedda, these women keep weapons, knives and pistols around them as emblems of danger and excitement, but their primary weapons are their tongues as they wittily spar with one another and the passive girl living with them, whom they have nicknamed "The Dove." Through the very fact of her youth, however, "The Dove" has the only true potential for danger and excitement and, for that reason, is the central object of their linguistic abuse and desire. Her retaliation—which in Ibsen would have become the subject of tragedy—is treated comically and wholly symbolically by Barnes, as the young boarder puts a bullet-hole through their "scandalous" painting of Venetian courtesans. Once again Barnes's action, which in this case occurs offstage, brings the battle of wit into a concretized and static image that completes the play.

The same pattern of linguistic sparring that results in a visual denouement occurs time and again in these early works: in *Kurzy of the Sea* the hero's love for the "unnatural" is transformed into a wholesome sexual drive as a mermaid, thrown back into the sea, metamorphoses (again offstage) into a barmaid; the sexual freedom espoused by the castaway couple in *Five Thousand Miles* is contradicted by the discovery on their uninhabited island of an "eggbeater," which belies their isolation from civilization and symbolizes the result of any proposed union between them; Gheid Storm's attempt to sexually storm the walls of Helena Hucksteppe's self-sufficient disinterest in him and other men is visually presented in *To the Dogs* by his vaulting through her window sill, and his failure is realized by his doorway exit. In short, what we see in these early plays are the roots of the tableaux and emblematic structures of the great *Nightwood* and *The Antiphon*.

In several of these plays, Barnes wipes away all action, and explores instead the dialogue of wit. In works such as *An Irish Triangle, Little Drops of Rain, Two Ladies Take Tea, Water-Ice*, and *She Tells Her Daughter*, Barnes returns to the Socratic dialogues, one of the roots of theater, in order to push away from a naturalist drama toward a theater in which language, as opposed to setting, character, or thematic structure, dominates. There is no true response possible to Shiela O'Hare's recounting of the sexual arrangement between her husband and the lady (and/or possibly the husband) of the manor house; Kathleen's bourgeois shock is simply a tool to keep the language and her story moving. Mitzi's outrage against Lady Lookover's dismissal of her and her generation in *Little Drops of Rain* simply spurs the witty maxims and homilies of the elder. The daughter's innocence in *She Tells Her Daughter* is merely a fact around which Madame Deerfont weaves the tale of her own murderous past. In these plays Barnes has stripped away action and setting in a manner that would be easily at home on the stage of Beckett, Albee, or Pinter. As Barnes biographer Andrew Field has suggested of Barnes's comedy of 1918, *Madame Collects Herself*, the play has less to do with influences of the time, particularly those of her fellow playwrights of the Provincetown group—Eugene O'Neill, Susan Glaspell, and Edna St. Vincent Millay—than it does with Eugene Ionesco.

Unsurprisingly, few critics of the day could make much sense of the plays of Djuna Barnes. While they all seemed to recognize something interesting was happening on stage (or, as Barnes bounded up and down the aisles, offstage), most reviewers were puzzled by the theatrical experience. Alexander Woollcott quipped of *Three From the Earth*, "[The play] is enormously interesting, and the greatest indoor sport this week is guessing what it means." Burns Mantle wrote of the same play: "It is probably the incalculable depth of the playlet that puts it beyond us. It is something that should be plumbed. But others must do it. We are a rotten plumber." Only S. J. Kaufman recognized Barnes's talent: "Miss Barnes' play is so near to being great that we hope that we shall be able to see it again. And we hope it's printed. ...Even now as we write the power, the simplicity and withal the incalculable depth of it has us enthralled."

Kaufman did get his wish. *Three From the Earth* was reprinted in *Little Review* and, subsequently, in both Barnes's *A Book* and in its republication as *A Night Among the Horses* in 1929. However, none of these plays has been reprinted since then, and one of them, *Kurzy of the Sea*, has never been published before. In its ongoing attempt to make the work of Djuna Barnes available, Sun & Moon is proud to have been able to bring this book into print.

I would like to thank the entire staff of Sun & Moon Press and, in particular, to express my gratitude to Tracy Biga, who copyedited these plays, Guy Bennett, who typeset and designed the internal contents of the book, and Elaine Crees-Piechowski. Susan Clark provided me early on with direction by allowing me to read her dissertation, *Misalliance: Djuna Barnes and the American Theatre*; and Philip Herring, Beth Alvarez, and the University of Maryland Library helped me obtain copies of missing plays. My thanks also to the Estate of Djuna Barnes and Herbert Mitgang of The Author's League Fund for allowing me to publish several of these scripts.

—DOUGLAS MESSERLI

THE DEATH OF LIFE

New York Morning Telegraph Sunday Magazine,
December 17, 1916.

Death Is the Poor Man's Purse.

—BAUDELAIRE

SCENE: *The semi-circle of a courtyard. Three doors open into it, a little to the left. To the right a glimpse of grass can be seen, interrupted by one of those small rooms with half the side cut out to permit of the selling of cheap sandwiches and penny coffee; a starved looking house like a mouth that must offer for sale that which it needs so badly for its own nourishment.*

A man stands before this house with his legs crossed; he holds a cup in one hand and a cheese sandwich in the other. He is portly and ill shaven. Above his coat collar a dirty handkerchief protrudes; he wears glasses with a thin silver chain looped behind the ear; his vest is red and has once been very evidently the pride of its owner, but the pride, along with this article of decoration, has faded down into a sort of bravado. When a proud man can no longer send his clothes to the laundry, he sends them to his ego.

As he drinks he looks from time to time at the door to the left. He does not seem particularly interested whether it opens or not, staring at it as something not to be worried about.

Presently shabby men begin forming a line opposite the coffee stand; gray men in gray clothes, with that rising hip that seems to be attempting to meet the pocket hugging hand. Some of them are lean, most of them are drunk, all of them are sad.

The door to the left opens and RAGNA *comes out.*

RAGNA: [*sitting down on the door step*] How goes it with you today, Toro, with the rain setting in between the stones like wet eyes?

TORO: [*drinking slowly*] Not good, not bad, that's the pity of it. A horse neighing in the gray streets at dawn is more cheerful than listening to the wind passing through the noses of the poor. And it's a long time, I'm thinking, it will be before it's good or ill for the likes of us that are of the seventies.

RAGNA: How, Toro?

TORO: It's many's the long day that I have seen over seventy cents the week for that which keeps a man from crying out like a frightened dog in a marsh.

RAGNA: You're not happy today, Toro, and the sky dropping down its rain on you and on the poor city grass that's born reluctant and old.

TORO: Nor it's you that's always happy, Miss Ragna. It's many's the time I've watched you coming out of your house of eve, with that look in your eyes is most pitiful to see—that look that means neither—good nor bad.

RAGNA: Life will change soon, Toro, and both of us will have plenty, for it's life is great and diverse.

TORO: Life is different for folks only in where they meet their loves and where they bury them.

RAGNA: I haven't met my love yet.

TORO: [*emptying his cup*] It's only a corpse that can be standard and it's only the morgue where equal attention fills the requirements of all.

RAGNA: [*half to herself, brushing the hair out of her eyes*]
I haven't met him yet, but some day I'll be seeing him
with these eyes that are mine, and some day I'll be
hearing him with these ears which are set like traps
for the coming of his feet, and some day with these
two hands I will be caressing him like he was a peaceful night where darkness is a cushion for the mind.

TORO: Aye, mayhap!

RAGNA: [*paying no attention to him*] And it's him will be
a fine king on a white horse, with gold running up his
trousers, and gold hanging down over his shoulders,
like tassels, and the mighty look in his face will be my
hope always.

TORO: Aye, aye.

RAGNA: And I shall say things that he will understand,
for I am artist and poet, and know the language surely
that reaches a man's heart when he is bravest and best.
And in the cold night I will make little blankets for his
heart with the touches of my palms, and I'll spread
him a net of fine gold hair that is mine. I'll cover his
sight with kisses that will comfort and confound. And
he shall arise like a mighty tree in a lonesome place.
Like ivy I'll cover his weakness always. With the vigilance of my leaves I'll hide him from the contempt of
lesser men.

TORO: You be chanting as a high priest, girl, and her-
rings going up two cents the pound in the markets,
and the shops ignorant of the sound of our feet these
long days past. The bread one eats lies down in one
like a debt one must pay. And the fire in the chimney
gone out leaving only a little smoke like a sneer.

RAGNA: I cannot be unhappy today. It's true that it's bread at five cents the loaf I have only, and it lasting two days, and tea that hasn't been whitened with milk since that last picture paid the rent six weeks ago. And it's many's the day I haven't eaten at all unless a friend took me out. And that's the worst, for when hunger is gone, so is the brain and the heart, sitting staring at a fool who never had anything to him but his hip pockets where coin is lying. Well, one must sell one's mind often to live at all.

TORO: It's hell, that's what it is!

RAGNA: It's pretty bad, when one loses one's heart one loses everything, and when one just lives, one dies inside, so the body becomes a little motion only wherein a thing has dropped on its knees and fallen forward. Look there—do you see? [*She points to one in the crowd.*] That look in his eyes is the corpse leaning a bit sideways against his forehead with dull weight.

TORO: Maybe you're happier than I, but you're more dreadful.

RAGNA: That's always so with us.

TORO: Why?

RAGNA: It's because you mean more than you say; we say more than we mean. [*She puts her chin in her hand.*] We're dreaming always and fancying things ahead so that you may be living them, so we have no time to be feeling them. It's a life in which one loses one's friends from borrowing, and keeps one's enemies.

TORO: It's a powerful thing you have been saying.

RAGNA: Aye, for it's I know and it's you that know. It's easier for you men; you can get a free lunch with your glass of beer, but a woman just has to do, or cadge. All you do not take from the world the world takes from you, all the flowering plants you have denied yourself are full of you, your presence makes the wheat fields uneasy, because of you and likes of you the markets are querulous and mean and overfed. The joints of beef you have not eaten have eaten you. They are glutted with the mouths they have left empty. Oh, food that was meant for my mouth, how desolate you have been! I can hear my share of the world complaining because my teeth are not set in it. My place in the world is crying with its emptiness. I can feel the breaths I have not breathed swelling out the world till it cracks!

TORO: And what will you be doing?

RAGNA: [*softly*] In the end I shall kill all that has been my life. First, I must find my king.

    One of the shabby men has edged up to the two as they converse, a cup of coffee in hand. He stands for a few moments staring first at one and then at the other. He is emaciated and in tatters, his thin nostrils quiver as though he experienced physical pain in drawing breath. His shoes are broken and show the toes where they merge from a thin-worn blue sock. His hair is wild and blond. He seems both interested and shy. He does not attempt to enter into conversation, drinking his coffee as they talk as though it made him happier.

TORO: [*sniffing*] People smell like their wages. I can tell how much a man makes by his perfume. The odor of agony is thick in this alley.

THE MAN: [*timidly*] Perhaps it's me.

TORO: [*without turning around*] I shouldn't wonder.

RAGNA: [*kindly*] You know, too, perhaps, how it is that we live on nothing? Well, it is simple enough. [*counting off*] Three cents worth of rolls and some tea that lasts the week; then there's milk that lasts a while also, and there's the sup when it hasn't sugar, and there's the bread when it hasn't butter. One sleeps late and one goes to bed late, and one manages somehow.

THE MAN: Do you live like that?

RAGNA: [*dully*] Like that.

THE MAN: Always?

RAGNA: Long enough to make us appreciate living otherwise; there's always a time when things change—for a little.

THE MAN: Now I would have said that I had a worse time of it than you, but I guess perhaps not; what with the free lunches and the bread lines and penny coffee stands and the work a man picks up a woman couldn't be doing, and then I suppose your ambitions stand in your way a bit, too.

RAGNA: [*looking at him for the first time*] Ambitions, what do you know of ambitions?

THE MAN: We all have them, miss—perhaps to some it is a long silk gown, and to others a garden by the sea. To me it might have been just enough tools to have kept at my trade.

RAGNA: Tools? Trade?

THE MAN: I'm a carpenter and cabinet maker, miss, and it takes many fine tools to live up to my imagination. [*with a touch of pride*] I don't like to be boasting, but it's many the bunch of grapes I have added to the chairs of the past, for furniture rejoices in its vintage the same as me and you, and chairs, like folk, must have their attention.

TORO: You're fanciful.

THE MAN: Nay, man; I have only a memory.

TORO: That's a way, with salaries, they do beget forgetfulness.

THE MAN: [*in an undertone*] And the little lady here?

TORO: An artist. A fine girl and bright, though it's little enough she has, I'm thinking, to make the smiles cross her mouth the way they have been doing when she sits alone there dreaming the while below the flowers of her window and beneath the vine.

THE MAN: It's a pretty face. Mostly artists?

TORO: Mostly, just you and me that ain't.

THE MAN: It's a bad life for a woman, but one gets used to little food and one learns to need less and keep quite healthy withal.

TORO: Aye; but I hate to see her dreaming there and talking of her king; girls only talk of their king when they have sighted their beggars.

THE MAN: Oh, it's nothing. This is like lining up before a cash window on pay day, only here the day's work is despair, and despair's pay is always small bread and the company of the shivering.

As they continue, they fail to notice that RAGNA *has arisen and gone in—at least* TORO *has failed to observe it.*

THE MAN: Strange, her bones were set like a tripod over the fires of life and youth and in the end—

TORO: There will be no end.

THE MAN: There is always an end; life affords life to

everything but its living. You see, I knew her well
[TORO *starts.*]; aye, aye, I pretended, that I might help
her always. I heard her talking about her king before
she saw me, and when she did—[*slowly his shoulders
rise and as slowly fall; he sets the cup down*] "And he
a fine king on a white horse, with gold running up his
trousers and gold hanging down his shoulders, and a
look in his face will be my hope always." [*He laughs,
lighting his pipe with that precision only customary
to habitues.*] "And he rising like a mighty tree in a lonesome place. Like ivy I'll cover his frailties, and with
the vigilance of my leaves I'll hide him from the contempt of lesser men." [*He laughs again.*]

TORO: Well, well, well; so this is what seventy cents a
week will bring a girl to.

THE MAN: She hasn't altered—and neither have I, only
in the matter of the place I lay my head, and the place
I do be watching the long nights for the rabbits in the
summer [*breaking off*]. And she'll carry all her fancies
and the lace of her heart into the outer darkness, there
to pluck and pluck until eternity shall cease—raveling
her past like an old relentless skein.

> *At this instant a shot is heard, a dull sound as of
> something heavy falling, and into the path at their feet
> drops a white rose.* TORO *leans down sharply, raising
> his eyes as he does so.* THE MAN *does not move.*

TORO: A flower has fallen, strangely broken, from Ragna's
window.

THE MAN: Do I smell powder?

TORO: [*fingering the rose sadly*] Poor little thing. Why
[*he examines its stem*], it has been shot off—wasn't

that a pistol? [*He stares at* THE MAN *for a second and then starts toward Ragna's door.*]

THE MAN: [*laying his hand on* TORO'S *arm*] Nay, man; let her be. Now that she has peace at last and her dream surely. Look you there! Do you see yon bunch of grapes hanging by a thread? They also felt her shot—so, they fall. [*He stoops over and picks them up, holding them at arm's length.*] What was it she said, "Everything we are denied lives in us, and some day I'll kill all my life that lives in other things only." [*He begins to weep softly.*] And it's music will be looking for its song, now she's dead, and it's many an eve will come down without color, now she's no more. Come, let us to the funeral.

TORO: [*in a frightened whisper*] Funeral! Suicide! Did you say Ragna had killed herself?

THE MAN: Friend, she shot life, life that was denied her; life that has lived on her until she died. And now the flower has fallen and the grape lies shattered—and there is no more of her than these things she might not keep.

TORO: But Ragna!

THE MAN: You and I hold all that's left of Ragna. [*lifting up the flower*] Ah, it was a kind face, yours, always. Look how her eyelids close. [His tears fall softly upon the withered thing.] And how her pale lips hold still a little open for the saying of the things only silence can hear. [*He puts the flower back into* TORO'S *hand, and touches the grapes.*] Ah, what a fine, proud spirit yours was, girl, and full of fire and faith and love always. And your feet making music on the pavements of a relentless town. Aye, it was a fine vintage you were, Ragna, at life's board, and it's a fine death you have. Come. [*He takes* TORO'S *unresisting arm.*] Let us go to the burying. [TORO *looks at him, but does not speak.*]

THE MAN: We will bury her deep beneath our hearts, yours and mine—for her soul is a flower, and that we may not touch; but her spirit is wine, and that we may drink, that she may have her shroud.

They pass out together into the dim green.

AT THE ROOTS OF THE STARS

New York Morning Telegraph Sunday Magazine,
February 11, 1917

Place:

Southampton, England. In an old basement.

Persons:

MAGEEN, who occupies the bed

MAZE, an old woman

TRAVNA, she who puts her head in at the door

SCENE: *The interior of a basement near the wharves. The plaster is beginning to show the veins that come with dampness. A little to the right of center stage a bed stands sideways: a high legged bed with white linen and ruffles of red and black chintz. At the one window at the back curtains of the same material, propped by a beer pail. There is a rag rug on the floor; a dresser with a few bits of jewelry, a picture of an old woman in a cap, evidently one of the older generation that we press upon the memory as a flower upon a book. A set of silver drinking mugs hang under the mantle that sports two gaudy green vases. There is about everything a sort of cleanly decay.*

On the bed MAGEEN *is lying in a gray and blue dressing gown that extends to the ankles, where it is taken up by a pair of heelless red slippers.* MAZE *stands by the window; she is of that indeterminate age between middle and youth, that we who look on speak of as "well preserved" if we have mentally placed her in the later forties, and as "ageing" if we have left her this side of thirty. Her face is large and quick with somber light; she is quite simple in her manner and her dress, while* MAGEEN *has to the contrary, an air of over-decoration not of alien objects, but of person.*

The flesh beneath her eyes has a decorative air; her hair is over-waved and caught with rhinestone combs. Two splendid earrings hang heavily in her ears, a case in which the ear seems to be worn for the benefit of the rings. Her laugh is at once loud and full of pleasure, with an undertone that hints biting sarcasm and bitter wit.

MAGEEN: Is it raining yet, child?

MAZE: Since the day before yesterday.

MAGEEN: Ah, ha, people no longer go to work with dry shirts; the boys going by in the early dawn are nothing but a line of wet wash. Well, it's them that are the happy ones, I'm thinking, with their pails of beer over their arms and their trade beneath their feet. I hear a great sound of building away to the west. What might it be?

MAZE: A new boat, a new house—who can tell?

MAGEEN: It is glad I am that there are men in the world who keep bracing the beams of the past and making things new the while—a glad woman I'd be, Maze, this day, and me with my veins swelling up like grapes, if it wasn't for the troubles of some of the friends I have.

MAZE: You speak as though you were a queen on a great throne instead of the landlady of a dirty inn that's stale with the cigar butts of the men of yesterday, and damp with the tears of women.

MAGEEN: Ah, true it is that our prayers are longer than our time to sin. So little time we have to ope our mouths; so short the space in which to kiss or kill; our life so badly spent in being that life's half. I so regret the tongue is of such insufficient length for the ridiculing of the world. Yet I am one of those women who come into it grand, and go out of it brave.

MAZE: Aye, you're well enough.

MAGEEN: I am that. [*turning over with perfect good humor*] What's the use of being otherwise? I am a heavy ship with my cargo of troubles, but I am riding easily, and will ride.

MAZE: Sometimes I'm thinking you have too much pride, with your light heart and your hopefulness.

MAGEEN: Child, child, what a young one you are, and you twenty years rolling about in the sun before I got half launched from the sling, but it's a little pebble you are and I a heavy stone, and you'll be but a pinch of dust when I am still an obstacle.

MAZE: You're a bitter thing; you'd better be sipping your beer instead of making fun of an old woman who counted her gray hairs before you had down to count, and was snapping her teeth before there were problems at all.

MAGEEN: Well, well, what of your girl Sarah today? It was a fine creature she used to be, full of the lust of ruined fields and the joy of life, and the birds flying behind her like moving embroidery against the sky, and she walking between them and the sun, making wine as she walked of the grass, the grain, and the dust.

MAZE: She's little enough now but a blond thing that has left the colors of her heart along the ways she has walked, so that her past is autumn and her face winter.

MAGEEN: [*dreaming*] I like to hear the hammers falling

there in the upper world with a sound to them as though they fell on wet wood, damp with the spray of an alien sea, and the gray brightness is an English day always, that lies thick and heavy on the lip, like a kiss is taken with tears beneath the eyelid.

MAZE: [*looking out of the window*] Mayhap it's a pier, a boat or a house they're building.

MAGEEN: It's getting chill, Maze, put a log on the fire. [*She puts her arms behind her head.*] It's a long time I've been lying here on my back beneath the world in this cellar, listening to the people all walking over my head, like a corpse that has flung the loam out of its ears and tossed the pennies from its eyes.

MAZE: It's no wonder you are sick always, and you beneath the house and beneath man, and hid from the stars.

MAGEEN: It's glad I am to be at the roots of the stars, for it's the roots get the truth. The sun coming out for a moment may deceive the flower, but the root know the lie.

MAZE: How long is it you have been staring at the ceiling here?

MAGEEN: Ever since Ulan went away, singing a great song and a fine, with the tommies trotting behind like a pinch of pollen that does be following the breeze. And it's here I'll be lying when he comes back again after learning life in this great street that ends in the arms of death. And it's a fine boy he will be when he comes back to tell me in words as profitable as the king's what's being done that's a glory to man in the world outside. Perhaps he has a woman who loves him.

For women need a great man to sing a little song above. Between the first button of the vest and the third have been played all the symphonies of life, by the straying hand of a woman.

MAZE: Perhaps she's a wench selling fish in the market place.

MAGEEN: So much the better. What one knows of the sea is well, if only by the taste on the tongue; all that's in life passes through us utterly. The flower through the gateways of our eyes; the fish and the fine fruits and the ripe wine by way of our mouth; every phrase is clothed in the winding sheet of some dead thing, and through the arches of our ears walks forever the music of creation. We are but a net, that quivers when the wind passes and shudders when the storm breaks, and in the end is torn utterly with nothing caught but the drift—wings of a bird, a petal, a dead sunbeam we call a shadow.

MAZE: Life is not like that at all; you're dreaming, Mageen. It's pitiless and hard, and it makes our children terrible and normal, and it makes our hopes dreadful and natural, and its sternness is very great, and its greatness very small.

MAGEEN: [*turning over again*] Woman, don't you suppose I know? It's only ten years I have put the world away and have lain in this basement listening to the feet of the universe passing over me. I remember well the dray-men in the streets selling their dirty fruit and their dry figs, and it's well I remember the old-clothes men handling their wares like ailments, for all dresses are scabs from the wounds of that strife we call a living.

MAZE: Aye, and what else do you recall?

MAGEEN: Men with their heads like bowls of vanity, set upon their necks, wherein eyes burn somberly that will so soon be ash. And the little girls running down past Wicklow's shop for a sight of the window where stood the wax doll that came from France; and it austere and chic, with its high piled hair and its small ribs pinched by old lace and Burgundy taffeta—ah, it's indeed well I remember—

MAZE: But wouldn't you like to see it all again, you could and you wanted to, with the help of the girl Travna, and a chair perhaps. Isn't it aching you are for a sound of the chatter of men?

MAGEEN: [*annoyed*] Why? For speech we are damned, are we not? The one word the donkey speaks has branded him an ass. Why should I bother looking into men's faces when their feet tell the truth for them, as the roots tell the truth of the day. A man may be looking on heaven, but if his feet are set on hell, they will give him away.

MAZE: Can you tell that?

MAGEEN: I can. Why do you suppose I should have had to listen to these years past; to the frying of the fat in the pans of my boarders; to the footfalls of those as pass over my head here? Come and listen; this part of the house is beneath the street and one can hear?

They both listen. The rhythmic sound of heavy traffic can be heard, the sharp staccato of high heels, the dragging step, the quick. Steps of the bricklayer, the sound of the thinker, the butcher, the poet.

Well, do you be hearing?

MAZE: But it tells me naught.

MAGEEN: [*smiling*] Because you have not listened, day on day, for ten long years, waiting for the step you know will come.

MAZE: Ulan's.

MAGEEN: Yes, I shall know when he comes.

MAZE: You don't remember?

MAGEEN: Not remember? I remember when he used to walk upon my heart before I gave him birth at all. And it's I who knew his footfall before his feet knew the ways of walking. Have I not listened to him coming in the stillness of the night, when we were only one. Like a vine his life crept at my side, and it's not the old tree will forget the young, that has sapped it of strength that it might stand, for an old tree is a glorious thing when it rises dead and gray, with the green leaves of its child shining upon it like the sun. It's not only to the level of the sound to which one should be lifted; one should be lifted to the level of the flesh. I am still a little proud of all that life can mean and cannot be.

MAZE: But after ten years?

MAGEEN: A son does not change his walk, any more than the leaves change their sound. Perhaps it's a quick wind, and perhaps it's a slow—the leaves sing the same always.

MAZE: But so many feet, and so much alike?

MAGEEN: You talk like those who have lived over-ground, not like those who have lived under, Maze. Who can deceive me in the cadence of the coming of my son? Not you, not the pavement, not time. I hope to hear the foot grown into the foot of a man, falling with the fire of purpose and the magnitude of this earth that takes us and uncurls us, and stretches us like the string of a harp, and lets time play upon us, and in the end smites us back into a circle of silence.

MAZE: But while you're talking he might come one day.

MAGEEN: It cannot be. Life is too quiet for my noise to be drowned. There is nothing under heaven or earth, or above it, that is sound excepting the crying of a child. That's why for some there is a great silence, filled with nothing but the throats of creatures not theirs, using the tongues that ring in earless space, and eyes that are little glasses turned toward the summit of your empty sky.

MAZE: I do not know.

MAGEEN: But it's I that know, and will know.

MAZE: All things are strange because we have known them always.

MAGEEN: [*irrelevantly*] Besides, he is a trifle lame. No one but I would mark it.

MAZE: But so many people are lame.

MAGEEN: I shall know. A mother does not overestimate, and he's the greatest of them all—my son, with the bonny light on his air always, and the ring in his voice that is like a page from a solemn book, and his purpose mighty, as the purpose of all who dream. He's a light I set burning twenty years ago, that was but a little candle then, but must be a blaze now, for the winds of strife have fanned it high, I know—ah it's much celebrating there will be the day Ulan comes. And it's I whose lips are shaken with the fermenting wine of faith, and it's I whose heart is great and glad, so that it lies upon the throat of my body like a diamond upon black cloth. [*suddenly*] Hark!

[*She rises upon her elbow, a light breaks slowly across her face, from eyes to mouth. She begins to tremble.*]

Ah, God, it's him, Maze; listen, do you hear?

[*A very faint sound as of some one passing slowly. A step a little uneven, as though one foot were dragging.*]

Quick, quick, tell Travna to bring him to me!

[MAZE *starts toward the door and exits in the middle of* MAGEEN'S *speech.*]

Ah, Ulan, I knew you would come back to me again out of the sky where I hung you with tears and with laughter; and it's I who knew some day you would turn to me, as the flower must return to the root. And it's I, your mother, Ulan, knew that those who called you wild would know you as good, and those who called you bonny would call you beautiful, and those who called you clever would hail you as noble. And it's I, your mother, Ulan, who knew that there was one road you would not walk without her knowing, and that the road of her exceeding expectancy and her impatient love.

She turns toward the door. At this moment the face of TRAVNA, *the maid, appears, her wide, pretty mouth half-open.*

TRAVNA: Ma'am, I can't bring him in.

MAGEEN: [*stretching half off the bed*] Why? Why?

TRAVNA: Because it's a donkey, ma'am.

MAGEEN: [*falling back upon the bed, slowly*] And it's I whose tears are too heavy for my eyes; they fall upon my breasts and crush them; they lie upon my sight, staggering drunkenly, and form a drop of curious and wet despair—spreading like a flood—as in a flood all but my laugh is drowned and broken like beaten grass—the terrible quietness of nothing that breaks the heart.

MAZE: [*returning, clasping and unclasping her hands*] The poor beast walked a little lame. They'd fettered him on the commons, too, where the grass is pale and thin.

MAGEEN: [*turning over*] It's getting chill. Is there aught left of the beer?

MAGGIE OF THE SAINTS

New York Morning Telegraph Sunday Magazine,
October 28, 1917

Persons:

MAGGIE, charwoman of a church
MARY O'BRIAN, her mother, an old woman
TWO ALTAR BOYS

Place:

The interior of an old church in a fishing village.

Time:

Nineteen hundred and sixteen.

SCENE: *The small door leads out into a sandy stretch of road that rises over a hill where wooden crosses and tombstones stand gray with age and leaning in the wind like the sails of the boats that their occupants once navigated. On either side of the oak settles at right and left of the church entrance are two tall cupboards. In one of them are a pile of hymn books, rosaries, Bible literature and old and faded prayer books belonging to children of the last century. In the other* MAGGIE'S *apron, brush and scouring rags. There is a billboard in the center, where church notices and baptisms are recorded.*

The pews are scrupulously clean, the floors shine with the devotions of the population and the brushes of MAGGIE. *Two blue-gowned angels stand erect and spotless in the niches on either side of the figure of the Holy Virgin.*

High up in the gallery, approached by a flight of rickety stairs, burns the halo of Christ, and away in the distance can be heard the chattering of children as the smoky, sweet-smelling incense hovers about the door undecided whether to enter the bright light of the waning day or to stay within the sanctuary.

MAGGIE *is a short, middle-aged woman. Her face*

is pallid and wrinkled. The blue eyes squint a little and the sharp nose terminates in a sudden round point descending sharply to a mouth both broad and good-natured. Her hair is light and dusty blonde, her hands are short, thick-knuckled, and the nails torn, black and broken—the charwoman's hand.

Her mother is an old, erect woman of ninety. Her nose is still well shaped and fine, like a lonely and beautiful fragment in the midst of a ruin. She rises and sinks on her knees now like one who exercises not the heart but the limbs.

A woman who in youth had looked at the styles as one looks at a lover, a woman who had been brought up in those broad channels that were at their zenith in eighteen hundred and eighteen, those days when people scorned any old religion or belief, either in art, literature or life. She was the daughter of a free thinker, an atheist, a philistine, and she lived half her life as such people would have her live it. Then the renaissance had come in eighteen hundred and thirty. People began to flock back to their hymn books, their prayer meetings, their superstitions; they began to look in garret and cellar for furniture of a mid-Victorian design; they adopted bustles and shunned everything for the life of a devotee and a believer.

Now her mother was too old to change. She was so old that she had forgotten the past, could no longer contain the passing beliefs of a transient middle age, and was incapable of grasping anything further. Therefore when this play opens the second renaissance found her incapable of understanding, of devotion or of re-

*jection. She was now only a passive bubble in the
draught that lay in the goblet of life.*

MAGGIE: [*on her knees, scrubbing*] It's fifteen years now
I've been servant of the Lord, and it's on my knees
I've been more often than any of you and for a clean-
lier trade. The sinners, too, why do they be coming
here at all? To get down and to pray to the Lord that
He may clean their dirty souls, is it? And me going
down year in and year out and rising up again for the
sweetening of the planks and the dusting of the pews,
and for the sweeping out and the arranging of the
household that praises the Lord I have served best.

MARY: [*in her corner, almost beyond the eye power of
her daughter*] And the Lord saith the mountains shall
drop down new wine and the hills shall flow milk, and
the rivers of Judah—

MAGGIE: [*scornfully*] Ah, but it's different these days,
old woman. It's little enough the mountains be dropping down and pitiful little milk we're having, and as
for Judah, she hadn't anything on me at all.

MARY: [*continuing*] Oh, praise the Lord who has dealt
wondrously with me and mine.

MAGGIE: Mother, I've been dreaming lately. [*She sits
up on her knees, looking toward the darkened corner
where her mother sits erect and praying, her face in
the air.*] Shall I be telling you? I dreamed that the day
of judgment was on us all, and that the graves out there
in the gloaming opened up, and all those as were our
sons and the sons of our sons walked, and the glory in
their faces was wonderful and holy, and they moved
like kings and made merry, and the smell of the sea,

where they did hard labor till they died, had gone from them; and the stench of the grave, where they rested, was all about them like an odor of idleness and ease; and they came all a-trooping down the road that leads into the church, and they were all singing.

MARY: [*startled out of her chant*] Eh?

MAGGIE: Aye, it's true. And there was Kit Borova, who died at sea, and the kid Michael, who was found drifting, and old Patrick Shank, who lay on the floor of the barroom some thirty years ago with a knife in his back. And now that knife was shining powerful and glorious like a decoration. And I dreamed that they entered the church, and they took their pews, and they lifted up their eyes, saying, "There is a new day in Cape Shawn now." And I stopped with my hands in the pail of water and I spoke to them. "It has been a long day you've been coming and a little wind in the grass to help you, and it's a doleful memory I have had of you all, but you're welcome to my house as I have cleaned as white as the throne and made as sweet as the Spring, and the Lord's blessing on you from now on. Amen." And they looked down at me, mother, and they prayed to me a little, bowing, and I said nothing for fear of making them ashamed of their mistake. But it was a grand dream, and I grow each day older dreaming it back to my heart again.

MARY: [*in a firm voice*] What is it you be saying, child? Dreams are the style now?

MAGGIE: I'm thinking perhaps they be.

MARY: [*folding her hands over her bodice*] How was it in the days when I was young? I should remember.

It's only the things one learns in youth that one can teach to youth. Other things are only tricks to keep you up to date. I'm thinking, but it's no use. My mind has been failing and failing till it's like moonlight in my head.

I don't remember anything, child, excepting my prayers, but to them I bring all of an old faith and all of an old decay, for youth is beautiful in what it learns and age in what it brings back in its heart to give once more into the hands of the mother from whom it took, so that it may be learned again.

MAGGIE: It's a sorrowful thing that you have lost track of yourself, mother. I'm thinking it was a grand youth you had and a fine middle age, but now you go about like a wind that is blown here and there, knowing no reason and finding no desire. And yet it's non-partisan you are at last, looking this way and that, saying, "Is it so, and is it not so," and never remembering the one or the other, or making good or evil of anything more in the world.

MARY: [*listening*] If one lives long enough it is as good as being a child again. There's some who say old age is bigoted and so it is, my dear, unless you outgrow yourself as I have done.

MAGGIE: You'll take the next change in beliefs with an open ear and an open eye and, more's the pity, with an open mouth.

MARY: Is a change coming?

MAGGIE: Perhaps, what can one know, and yet I think a dream like mine means something.

> *She gets up, moves her pail and brush to one side*

43

and begins dusting the little images. The altar boys can be seen in the vestry room, arranging a new pile of incense.

MARY: [*crossing herself*] Sorrow is in my heart that I have no memory with which to condemn that which must be sinful—for change is sinful always after twenty.

MAGGIE: [*wearily*] Well, I've been a faithful servant always, seeing the dawn and the evening from my knees and never missing one day in fifteen years, and it's a pension I should be receiving ere long, I'm thinking, and a little nodding in the street from men.

MARY: I'll bow to you, child, if it's a little recognition you're wanting. [*She begins to nod like a very old woman, and she mutters as she nods.*]

MAGGIE: It's not much help your nodding will be to me, mother. You've got past knowing what I was, or what I am—you forgot me while you bore me, and I'd slipped your memory while yet I was to be.

MARY: Are you saying hard things to the old, Maggie?

MAGGIE: No, I'm only telling you that you will never see this day your eyes are open on, nor hear what you yourself are saying more, but there's a smell in the air that I'm not too old to recognize and I know that there's a change coming somewhere, perhaps from the bowels of the earth and perhaps from the heavens—perhaps in a long line of the dead and perhaps in something that shall be new born on a Monday and me working here will not know of until the crier comes screaming the news. [*She finishes the idols and turns to the saints.*] I had day dreams once myself without sleeping. I thought I was to be a great lady with town folk bowing down to me in my beauty and my wealth and making little speeches in their mouths that would be a decoration to me as the knife to the back of Patrick Shank. And I thought that there would be a dress of silk and a slipper or two for my feet and an hour for doing nothing besides the hour for lunch. And that perhaps there was some one waiting for me somewhere who would speak the words of love that are grand, they say, and beautiful, and that I myself would be fair and great enough to scorn them when they came newest, not as I am now, too gray and pitiful and sad to scorn a declaration with all the poetry left out. And in those days, mother, I thought that perhaps in all the land and through all the coasts my name would be one that would bring tears into the eyes and praise into the throats. But I was a fool and I was born too soon—or too late.

MARY: You were born on a good day, child, on the saints' day, and there should be little complaining.

MAGGIE: Since then there's been little glory for me, or happiness that I didn't foresee myself in a glass of grog and it's only hard times and dirt that has been my lot and old age and pains coming upon me all through my veins, and they lie on me like hot and dreadful vines and they bulge out like terrible and bitter flowers where my legs have given service to the house-cleaning of the saints, for it's the varicose veins that will be my undoing.

MARY: Is this unrest the style now, child?

MAGGIE: What do styles matter, mother? Is that all you have learned in ninety years or no? I don't know; I guess the styles won't change till both of us be below ground deep enough not to notice the difference in the tread of feet.

MARY: The tread of feet?

MAGGIE: Free feet and slave feet.

MARY: There were only one kind in my day.

MAGGIE: You were born a free woman, but you know nothing now of it.

MARY: They were grand days, daughter, and I could recollect them.

MAGGIE: [*going down the side with scrubbing brush and soap*] Ah, well, if it weren't for me, how would all the saints be kept tidy and dusted at all, and their haloes shining brightly like a firefly in a lone and dark eve, and their gowns laid straight and crisp and neat for them—for I've not only been the wardrobe mistress of the Lord, but his charwoman and his servant always, and it's because of me and the likes of me the world over that there's something grand and clean and beautiful about them, and because of me and my kind that they are worshipped.

MARY: Are you speaking blasphemy or poetry? It's hard put to it I am to know these days.

MAGGIE: It's the greatest poetry I'm telling you, and the most wondrous thing in the world of labor.

MARY: Perhaps, maybe, I'll pray a little for safety. [*She prays once more, with her face in the air.*]

MAGGIE: [*unheeding*] And if it's pails and brushes that I have mucked with my whole life, then it's some recognition I should be getting, I'm thinking; for there's times a body is too tired to save the meanness of their work with little words of beauty and gentleness. And there's many's the night I sit looking out of my window into the graveyard wondering when I too will return to dust that I have been fighting fruitlessly all my days, with no one doing me praise at any time.

MARY: Blessed be—

MAGGIE: Them as are humble, as I am humble when I am rested. But there's hours when I have nothing but bitterness coming all through me like a stain—and strong tea and bitter coffee and wine do nothing for it at all, but make it grow and grow until I'm afeared.

MARY: And in the days to come, Lord, will your justice be on both men and women and on little children, and the lambs of the field that run among the grass like white fog—

MAGGIE: [*in the distance, near the altar*] Aye, pray away; little enough good that will do for me.

MARY: Little God, I am praying to you.

MAGGIE: And I am praying always, too, for one thing or another, but mostly for myself, I fear, for I'm a proud woman, though I'm always down upon my knees soaping and scrubbing and cleaning and getting the dust in my eyes and the same in my throat, and the both of them watering so that I can't see for tears, nor speak for the great difficulty it brings upon me.

MARY: [*folding her hands and looking away into the dim recess where the faint outline of the altar can be seen*] Here's a prayer from the very most of me that's left.

MAGGIE: And that nothing but a proud mist. [*She turns about on her knees, her arm in the pail of dirty water. In the distance behind her two small altar boys with torches are seen slowly ascending the stairs that lead to the gallery.* MAGGIE *calls out to them sadly.*) Be waiting a moment, children. I've taken away the image to dust, for I've neglected it these ten days past.

They do not hear her and turn the winding staircase and are lost to view.

MARY: [*suddenly, in a loud voice, looking straight ahead to the figure of* MAGGIE *on her knees*] Ah, Glory be, and are you here, and have you answered my prayers, and is it the miracle or is it the Judgment Day?

[MAGGIE *looks up, her mouth ajar.*]

Oh, wonderful day, oh most blessed of women, am I to have seen you come to earth again for the comfort of my last hours before I die. I'm full dumbfounded; but I'll make haste to pray to you a little. [*She slides to her knees, praying to* MAGGIE.]

MAGGIE: [*in a whisper*] Is it looney she is surely? [*Looking around her—at her pail, her brush and her draggled shirt; raising her eyes she sees the smallest boy reach out and light the halo above the empty niche. A wild, happy look comes into her eyes—her large mouth broadens, then she stares with a fixed expression at the open door.*)

[*quietly*] It has come.

The two children's voices are heard as they descend again.

THE TWO CHILDREN: I don't care, it was my turn. I say it wasn't. You have always had your way, now it's my turn to make the light—and besides, Father Fennell said—

A PASSION PLAY

Others (February 1918)

Persons:

FIRST THIEF

SECOND THIEF

SARAH, first prostitute

THEOCLEIA, second prostitute

THIRD FIGURE

GUARD

Place:

Calvary

Time:

In the days of Christ

SCENE: *The hillside. To the left a clump of bushes, to the right a dark wood. In the middle distance, two crosses. A glow from the city casts a shallow light on the foot of the hill.*

THEOCLEIA *is a Greek. Very blond with long legs and narrow shoulders. Her skin is but a thin veil over the veins of her flesh. The eyebrows and the slight down on her upper lip are so faint as to give the impression of something that has been marked on the reverse side. She is gay and heavily abandoned.*

SARAH *is a thin, small Jewess with tiny breasts, dark and curling hair, nose equiline, mouth large, teeth flat and fine. She has the arched swift eyes of a trotter. She has a trick of running her hand over her breasts and up to her throat. A perverse woman, whose knees move beneath her thin dress like spheres ascending and descending.*

FIRST THIEF, *a shaggy man of forty with long ragged moustache, small red eyes, a large Adam's apple and thin neck bones.*

SECOND THIEF, *a broad-faced blond, minus eyebrows, has broken arches and swallows incessantly.*

FIRST THIEF *breaks out of the bushes in pursuit of* SARAH, *the* SECOND THIEF *in pursuit of* THEOCLEIA. *They roll in a heap in the foreground.*

FIRST THIEF: [*wiping his mouth*] This moment's anticipation has upset my saliva for the last twenty-four hours. Come, kiss me. [*He kisses* SARAH.]

SECOND THIEF: [*his arm about* THEOCLEIA] You should treat a man better than that, who knocks at all the tavern gates on the way to hell this night.

SARAH: How now?

FIRST THIEF: [*shrugging his shoulders*] What matter's it, girl; beneath these whiskers is a mouth of splendid grossness—one cannot kiss all things unless one has the range.

SECOND THIEF: Waste not time, my friend, each minute grows a minute short in which to love.

THEOCLEIA: [*tucking up her gown*] Let us play then. You sit here and I there, if it's only a little time for life left to you. What is your offense?

FIRST *and* SECOND THIEF: Misconstruing the meaning of right and wrong.

SARAH: [*playing with* THIEF's *arm*] And you, what are you charged with?

FIRST THIEF: That fair sin called guilt, of that dear moment termed evil; I suffer the malady dubbed distemper and commit those follies spoken of as breach of law. And who make the laws, tell me? Some man, who, lacking my capacities, envied my life.

SECOND THIEF: What does it matter. We all end. Some die early and some when they are old; some when their sap is loose and some when their joints complain endlessly, "Enough, enough." But let us pinch and wrestle in that game they call the height of passion. There's that in me could smear the world with new voices calling out, "Forever and forever!"

THEOCLEIA: You are a dirty ruffian, but I like the odor of your filth, 'tis healthy.

SARAH: And I the odor of your breath, for through it blows the breaths of all things—some evil and some none too good.

They embrace each other. There is a short silence.

FIRST THIEF *to* SECOND: We are the common pools in which the refuse is flung. In which the child dips its feet, in which the horse sluices its nostrils, in which the sparrow cools its legs, in which the entrails of fish are thrown, through which runs the blood of a day's burst veins and the shucks of an hour's sucked fruit. The amazing gutter in which the world casts its wash and then cries, "'Tis muddy."

THEOCLEIA: And I come from a place that's overrun with things. Yet what can you do? Drive a rat into a corner, rascal, and all that's left for it is the knowledge of the corner's contour and, then, on to death.

SARAH: [*fondling the cheek of lover*] How shaggy you are, yet I know of a shaggier place, where nothing stirs, save the odor of flesh and of boots tossed among the catch; and no bird flung upward singing, with the earth upon its feet.

SECOND THIEF: Where come you from, what have you left undone?

SARAH: From handling men as if they were tripe, and the world a stew, and one the meat, and one the root, and one the thyme; and only a few spectators tasting with the wine still wet upon their teeth.

FIRST THIEF: All people have appetites, but few have stomachs. [*laughs as he picks fleas out of the hairy calves of his legs*]

THEOCLEIA: And do you die today or tomorrow? Has time passed, or is it on the road behind you?

SECOND THIEF: I know not, but there's evil in the air when a tree or a cross rears up. For one there's the nest to hatch out crows, and for the other nails to hatch out death.

FIRST THIEF: It's time for kisses, my girl; give me your fine wet mouth. [*kisses her, swaying a little*] I'm sure we hang this night for there's that done in the world that we are the father of, and no man escapes this city.

SARAH: Can you not fly?

THEOCLEIA: Or hide?

FIRST THIEF: [*sneering*] Or make excuses?

SECOND THIEF: [*in the same tone*] Or appeal to justice?

SARAH *and* THEOCLEIA: And why not?

FIRST THIEF: Because justice is not made for thieves, my girl, nor yet for prostitutes. I would tell you something, but lend me an ear.

SARAH: Speak on.

The scene grows dark, as if a storm were brewing. Only the silhouettes of the four heads and shoulders can be distinguished, and the form of the crosses.

FIRST THIEF: The world has two things—good and evil. The one passes through the city as the deer through the forest and people pay tribute to it, lawyers grow callouses on their heels over it; preachers lose the tips of the tongues exalting it—for it is pleasant and to the nose very gratifying, for it hath no odor. Thus it passes, smiling and in favor—'til puff [*snaps his fingers*], suddenly some one cries, "Carrion!" The world is suffused with the smell of flesh and sweat and the hot nausea of things that have died with fur on them, and things that have died naked and in gestures. And the lover with his nose in his mistress' throat, and the steer with his nostrils among the wrinkled bristles of his mate—perceive that there is an aroma in the air; a foul and penetrating stench; a thing that makes the breasts of woman bound, the tongues of men shed saliva and the mouths of those but lately smiling, draw in fear. We, my dears, are that stench.

THEOCLEIA: [*sadly*] We are to the world what the odor is to the flesh—and they cannot wash us out.

FIRST THIEF: [*grinning*] They do not want to wash us out, that would prove the stain their own; instead they kill us—thus—they put ourselves upon us.

THEOCLEIA: [*quietly*] I come from a strange place. [*points toward the city*] It is like a large room, it is full of shadows and great bright lights, and there are the garments of men and women, and leather moist from a waist, and gloves dirty from a journey, and there's a shift thrown over the antlers of a dead thing, and there are two stark rabbits, and between them is a glass of wine, an apple and a flower. And there's the sound of laughter and of tears dropping down solemnly from a high wet palate, and there is the murmur of hands passing over mouths, of limbs passing over limbs, of sighs mingling with sighs. And there's a shadow that has its security in the highest part of the room, and it swings back and forth upon the floor eternally, like the lunge of love. [*shudders*] And through it all somebody, sitting straight and dispassionate, speaks, saying: "Continue." And so I know nothing's over and nothing done.

FIRST THIEF: [*leaning forward*] You saw that?

SARAH: What was it?

SECOND THIEF: Heaven?

SARAH: Hell?

THEOCLEIA: [*bitterly*] Heaven has jelled and hell is rusty, and the doves of peace lie mangled and moulting in the rain. But I, I am young and cry forever, "On and on!"

SECOND THIEF: Truly, women are wonderful. A man commits a little thing and dies therefore; a woman all things and lives not till then. They are the tablets on which we write, "We have been."

SARAH: There is something leaden in the air. Nothing moves save what we cannot see; and the feet of all things are heavy on the earth; and the eyes of all things are wide and startled; and every tongue is in its cheek. Yet there's one string that, cut, would loose the world like a bag of feathers.

FIRST THIEF: You make me cold. My heart fails me. What was that?

[*All are quiet listening. Then whispers.*]

The dawn's coming, and we have lived at least a part of another day—come!

Two heads disappear.

SECOND THIEF: Theocleia, could you love me for an hour?

THEOCLEIA: We do not love in our trade—it is forbidden—after the first.

SECOND THIEF: Yet there's something healthy about a

man who has the malady of sin upon him. It tastes well beneath the tongue and sits easily upon the hips. Come, lift me up for an hour, as one heaves up a kitten.

The last two heads disappear. There is no sound save that of the faint rustling of leaves, the wind in the grass and the movement of animals. Presently the light begins to dawn faintly in the East. Now there are three crosses instead of two. The lights of the city have gone out. The momentary darkness must represent the passage of several hours—those between dusk and dawn. From the woods on the one side and the bushes on the other SARAH *and* THEOCLEIA *appear, crawling on hands and knees, until they reach that spot in which they were originally.*

SARAH: Theocleia!

THEOCLEIA: Sarah!

SARAH: Come!

THEOCLEIA: What have you?

SARAH: [*thrusting her hand into her bodice, bringing out dice*] Dice—let us toss for it.

THEOCLEIA: How much did he give you?

SARAH: Seven silver pieces—and you?

THEOCLEIA: I never bring as much—only six.

SARAH: Perhaps six is what he died for. Are they dead?
    [*They turn their faces toward the crosses.*]
    Look! There hangs a third. What a little flaming thing! Who is he? What has he done?

THEOCLEIA: It cannot have been much—he was not among us last eve.

SARAH: And who is that still more shadowy than the dead, that walks against the sky?

THEOCLEIA: That is the guard. [*She sits up, sniffing the air.*] What has gone out of the air? It is not the same consistency.

SARAH: It is simple, the air has cleared off. [*They begin to toss.*]

THEOCLEIA: Seven!

SARAH: Nine. And mind, you, I get the loin cloth of your little rascal if I throw double fives. It will make a pretty hanging, and there's that on it they say a man draws when he dies a violent death. And later we can say: "Thus our children would have looked."

THEOCLEIA: Four!

SARAH: Nine!

THEOCLEIA: Three!

SARAH: Double fives.

[*curtain*]

MADAME COLLECTS HERSELF

Parisienne, VI (June 1918)

Persons:
MONSIEUR GOUJON, barber
LULU, (MADAME GOUJON), manicurist
MADAME ZOLBO, patron
FIFINE, hairdresser
Place:
The Avenue.
Time:
Late afternoon.

SCENE: *The interior of a hairdressing parlor. Curtained compartments to the right and left. A manicure table, several pictures depicting very refined women smiling in front of swirls and puffs of hair, long braids and chignons, bangs and waterfalls. At side front is a counter for the display of puffs, wigs, combs and lotions.*

MADAME ZOLBO—*A stout, slightly pompous woman of forty odd, with high piled hair upon which rests an enormous velour hat supporting a bird of paradise. Her thick little feet are spatted and disappear beneath a buff and black sporting skirt. Her short hands with well-fed, Roman characteristics lie across her sable muff in jewelled complacency, while a red plush coat hangs sprawling like a cataract of blood over her arm. Every now and again the head of* MONSIEUR GOUJON *appears between the curtains. He is a middle aged man with romantic tendencies ending in fine whiskers and luxuriant hair. He wears his whiskers as the earth wears its hedges—consciously and decoratively.*

MADAME ZOLBO: [*cheerfully*] Good afternoon, Fifine, and you, Lulu. Can you curl and manicure me immediately? I haven't a moment. The Baroness does like to break bread on time. [*She moves forward into one of the compartments facing front, and begins divesting herself of wraps.*]

FIFINE: [*removing pins from* MADAME'S *hair*] Is this one of Michael's days?

MADAME ZOLBO: [*sadly*] Yes, it is his anniversary—I always wear him on Wednesdays, they are my days out. Give him to me. [*She takes the removed false curls from* FIFINE *and begins to stroke them.*] How well I remember how these curls looked on him, a most talented and melancholy man, just the right pallor and dignity, a little languid, perhaps, but his hair, as you can see for yourself, was the hair of an angel. It used to touch my cheek [*sighs*] so often in those fiery days before he passed beyond.

LULU: [*dipping* MADAME'S *hand in castile suds*] Dead!

MADAME ZOLBO: Dead! Died on the way home from "Boris"—would sing the finale up to the last moment.

FIFINE: [*testing the irons against her cheek*] You must have felt dreadfully.

MADAME ZOLBO: It almost killed me, yet I can say that I am never quite so proud as when I bear the honey-colored cylinders from that departed head.

FIFINE: [*curling*] Yes?

MADAME ZOLBO: Shaw says—I'm perfectly sure it's Shaw—that a woman is only what a man, or men, make her, and I admit that I am never so brilliant as when Michael lies curled in a sublime gesture on my forehead. [*twisting the curl over her eye*] Lay him a little sideways, he always looked well when reclining sideways and speaking of his soul.

LULU: [*bored*] He was the impetuous one?

MADAME ZOLBO: No, no, you are thinking of Conrad. [*sighing*] It was he, my dears, who gave me a pint of his blood when I lay at death's door in Aix-les-Bains one day last summer. Yes, one pint of an anarchist's blood flows in my veins. [*brusquely*] But it's safe with me.

FIFINE: [*closing one eye*] Madame has enough blue blood to overcome it. [*stifles a yawn*]

MADAME ZOLBO: [*amicably*] Blue blood, my dear, has its origin not in fine descent and careful selection, but in a certain strength that can keep all dangerous blood out of the joints.

FIFINE: [*beginning on left side*] High or low, Madame?

MADAME ZOLBO: Curl it high. I am dining tonight with the Baron, though I say safely enough that he has contributed less toward making me what I am than any other one person. This little square of skin that you may have noticed upon the upper right arm is his, my dears; it takes the place of a most annoying mole. It is a point with him to renew my failing youth.

LULU: [*sourly, pinking* MADAME's *fingers*] Madame looks upon men as cosmetics.

MADAME ZOLBO: [*with perfect humor*] They are the very breath of life.

    MONSIEUR GOUJON *enters.*

MONSIEUR GOUJON: Madame is happy today. [*taking pins and comb from* FIFINE] I will dress Madame's hair myself.

LULU: [*not looking up*] You are a little slow with that puff, Monsieur Goujon.

MONSIEUR GOUJON: [*glancing sideways at his wife*]
Patience, my dear.

FIFINE: A little brilliantine, Madame?

MADAME ZOLBO: Just a little.

LULU: The other hand, Madame.

MADAME ZOLBO: [*giving the other hand*] Be careful
with that index finger, it is not mine—well, of course,
I mean it wasn't mine. It belonged to General Pfiffing,
and it is the identical one with which he pointed toward the rising sun as he cried, "Onward to victory." It
has always done as much for me. Ah, but it was a delicate operation—that was a generous man!

MONSIEUR GOUJON: [*growing crimson*] This is something new?

MADAME ZOLBO: [*shrugging her shoulders*] Not so
very.

MONSIEUR GOUJON: [*very pale*] What do you mean?

MADAME ZOLBO: [*composed*] Monsieur Goujon, you
tremble! [*laughs softly*]

MONSIEUR GOUJON: [*in a jealous rage, with horror
added, to* FIFINE] Kill that woman! [*points to* MA-
DAME ZOLBO]

FIFINE: [*complacently*] Certainly, Monsieur. [*thrusts the
curling irons through* MADAME ZOLBO's *heart*]

MADAME ZOLBO: Goujon, you are always so tempera-
mental and hasty—not thus— [*She holds up her hand,
and then turning to* LULU *with a little bow.*] My heart,
Madame—pardon, but that is your husband's.

FIFINE: [*fanning the fainting* LULU, *but speaking of*
MADAME ZOLBO] What shall we do with her?

MONSIEUR GOUJON: [*furiously twirling his mous-*

tache] It depends. Where are you, Madame, in what spot are you yourself?

MADAME ZOLBO: Ah, Monsieur, that is a very elusive thing. Can I call it my soul, a blithe atom, a canary at song in the wilderness of my body?

MONSIEUR GOUJON: [*turning to his wife*] This is a woman's job. Strip her of her gifts, unravel the horrid spool until we reach the end—let us see what she is like.

MADAME ZOLBO: In vain! [*A strange light comes into her eyes—now almost the bright, round, all-seeing eyes of a bird. She makes no resistance.*]

　　LULU *and* FIFINE *slowly remove the golden puffs belonging to Michael the poet; they cut off Pfiffing's finger, next they strip the skin of the Baron away, and making a neat incision in her wrist draw one pint of blood—that pint donated by Conrad the anarchist. As the last drop descends into the manicure bowl* MADAME ZOLBO *disappears and a blond canary rises up toward the ceiling.*

MONSIEUR GOUJON: Ah, so—where is the Grand Dame now? Nothing but a hoarse-voiced sparrow! Come, my dear, weep no longer, we are better in this world for a woman less. [*to* FIFINE] Catch that bird and hang it beneath my sign that the world may see how I, Monsieur the barber, revenges himself. [*to* LULU] I give you back my heart as one takes a watch out of pawn.

FIFINE: [*closing the cage door on the canary and stepping out to hang it beneath the sign*] Still it is too bad. [*coming back*] She tipped so well.

MONSIEUR GOUJON: She was a fiend—she was worse than Salome—more horrible than Messalina. They gave, she took. Every time she returned home from a day in the world, her spaniel barked at some little strangeness she brought back with her. It is well, it is just.

FIFINE: [*near the door, crying out*] Look, look! [*She darts back excitedly.*] Monsieur, down on your knees. The bird's the Madame again—she grows larger and larger every minute; three men are already lying dead beneath her cage, and she is smiling and making ringlets over her fingers!

MONSIEUR GOUJON: [*resigned*] Heat the irons!

THREE FROM THE EARTH

Little Review, VI (November 1919)

Three from the Earth was first presented at the Provincetown Playhouse in New York, October 31, 1919, with the following cast:

JOHN CARSON	Ward Roege
JAMES CARSON	James Light
HENRY CARSON	Cesare Zwaska
KATE MORLEY	Ida Rauh

Setting by James Light.

Persons:
    JAMES, HENRY and JOHN, CARSON brothers
    KATE MORLEY, an adventuress, a lady of leisure
Time:
    Late afternoon.
Place:
    KATE MORLEY's boudoir. A long narrow room, with a great many lacquer screens in various shades of blue, a tastefully decorated room though rather extreme.

At the rise of the curtain the three Carson brothers are discovered sitting together on a couch to the left. They look like peasants of the most obvious type. They are tall, rather heavy——and range in age from nineteen to twenty-five. They have sandy, sun-bleached hair that insists upon sticking straight up—oily, sweaty skins—large hanging lips and small eyes on which a faint whitish down moves for lashes. They are clumsy and ill clothed. Russet shoes are on all six feet. They each wear a purple aster and each has on a tie of the super-stunning variety—they have evidently done their best to be as one might say "well dressed."

When they speak—aside from their grunts—their voices are rough, nasal and occasionally crack. They are stoop-shouldered and their hands are excessively ugly.

Yet in spite of all this, their eyes are intelligent, their smiles gentle, melancholy, compassionate. And though they have a look of formidable grossness and stupidity, there is, on second observation, a something beneath all this in no way in keeping with this first impression.

JOHN, the youngest, and the smallest, looks around the room carefully.

JOHN: A nice room, eh? [*He tries to whisper, but it comes forth buzzing and harsh.*]

JAMES: A woman's room.

HENRY: How?

JAMES: A narrow room, John.

JOHN: Well?

JAMES: Cats and narrow walls.

HENRY: [*grunting*] Ugh.

JOHN: Hush—I hear her coming! [*The curtains part and* KATE MORLEY *enters. She is a woman of about forty. Handsome. Dark. She is beautifully dressed—in a rather seductive fashion. She has a very interesting head; she has an air of one used to adulation and the pleasure of exerting her will. She has a trick of narrowing her eyes. As she comes forward there is a general commotion among the brothers, but none manages to stand up.*]

KATE: Good day, gentlemen.

ALL THREE: Good day.

KATE: Nice of you to call on me. [*She seats herself, crossing her legs.*] You are the three Carsons, John, James and Henry, aren't you? I haven't seen you for years, yet I think I should have known you.

ALL THREE: Ah ha.

KATE: Yes, I presume I should have known you. I have a good memory. Well, as I said, it's nice of you to come to see me. Social?

HENRY: You might call it that.

KATE: It's quite nice to get an unexpected visitor or so. I'm the kind of woman who knows just who is going to call on Monday, Tuesday, Thursday—

ALL THREE: Ah ha.

KATE: How's the country?

JOHN: Just the same.

KATE: It always is. Don't you go mad—watching it?

HENRY: Now and again.

KATE: And how's your father? [*not pausing for an answer—almost to herself*] I remember—*he* was always mad. He used to wear a green cloth suit, and he carried white rats all over his shoulders. [*remembering the three*] Ah, yes, your father—he was a barber, wasn't he?

HENRY: No, a chemist.

KATE: [*laughing uneasily*] I have a bad memory after all. Well, anyway, in those days he had begun to be queer—every one noticed it—even that funny man who had those three flaxen-haired daughters with the thin ankles who lives at the end of the street—And your mother—a prostitute, I believe.

HENRY: [*calmly*] At times.

KATE: A dancing girl without a clean word in her vocabulary, or a whole shirt to her name——

JAMES: But a woman with fancies.

KATE: [*sarcastically*] And what ability?

HENRY: Oh, none, just a burning desire.

KATE: What's the use of going into that? How did you get here—what for?

ALL THREE: On bicycles.

KATE: [*bursting into laughter*] How exactly ridiculous and appropriate—and what else?

JOHN: To see how the sun falls in a place like this.

KATE: [*angrily, rising*] Well, you see, from left to right, and right to left—

HENRY: True.

JOHN: [*quietly*] And we wanted to see how you walked, and sat down, and crossed your legs—

HENRY: And to get father's letters.

KATE: Well, you see how I walk, sit down, cross my legs. What letters?

JAMES: Letters to you.

KATE: [*uneasily*] So you know about that—well, and what would you fellows do with them—read them to see how clever they are?

JAMES: No, we have the clever ones.

KATE: Mine?

JOHN *and* HENRY: [*nodding*] Exactly.

KATE: Oh!

JOHN: You suffer?

KATE: From time to time—there's always a reaction.

HENRY: That's vulgar, isn't it?

KATE: Not unusually.

JOHN: The letters?

KATE: [*to herself*] Well, there is malice in me—what of it? We've all been a while with the dogs, we don't all learn to bark.

JOHN: Ah ha.

KATE: See here, what will you do with your father's letters?

HENRY: Destroy them, perhaps.

KATE: And if I give them to you—will your father be as generous with mine?

HENRY: Father is undoubtedly a gentleman—even at this moment.

KATE: Well, we shall see about that—first tell me how you live.

JOHN: We go down on the earth and find things, tear them up, shaking the dirt off. [*making motions to illustrate*] Then there are the cows to be milked, the horses—a few—to be fed, shod and curried—do you wish me to continue?

KATE: Yes, yes, go on.

HENRY: [*taking the tale up*] We get up at dawn, and our father turns over in bed and whispers: "If you meet any one, say nothing; if you are asked a question, look stupid—"

KATE: I believe you.

JAMES: And he says: "Go about your work as if you had neither sight, speech nor hearing—

KATE: Yes—

JOHN: And he adds: "If you should meet a woman in the road—"

KATE: [*excited*] Then what?

HENRY: That's enough. Then of a Sunday we watch the people going to church, when we hear the "Amen," we lift a little and sit back—and then again—

KATE: Religion?

HENRY: Enough for our simple needs.

KATE: Poor sheep!

JAMES: Wise sheep!

KATE: What! Well perhaps. No one is any longer sure of anything. Then what?

JOHN: When we come home he says: "What have you seen and heard today?" He never asks, "What have you said?"

KATE: He trusts you?

JOHN: Undoubtedly. Sometimes we say, "We saw a hawk

flying," or, "A badger passed," and sometimes we bring him the best treat of all—

KATE: Well?

JOHN: Something dead.

KATE: Dead?

HENRY: Anything that has destroyed the crops—a mole—a field-mouse.

KATE: And never anything that's harmless?

JOHN: Never.

KATE: Well, see here. I'll give you those letters. Suddenly my heart says to me, "Kate, give the oxen the rope, they won't run away."—Isn't it so? Very well, I put my hand on a certain package and all is over—I'm about to be married, you know. [*She has risen and gone over to a little box standing on the desk. Out from this she takes a package of letters tied with a red ribbon. She turns and walks straight up to* JOHN.] I'll give them to you. You are the youngest, the gentlest, and you have the nicest hands. [*She sits down, breathing with difficulty.*]

JOHN: [*putting them into his blouse*] Thank you, Kate Morley.

KATE: Now, tell me about everything. How is that mother of yours? I remember her—she was on the stage—she danced as they say, and she sang. She had a pet monkey—fed it honey out of a jar kept full by her admirers: grooms, stage hands, what not—

HENRY: Yes, and she used to draw pictures of it in the style of Dürer—almost morbid—and later it caught a disease and died—

KATE: I don't doubt it—and she, she had an under-lip

like a balloon—and your father kissed that mouth, was even tempted—

JAMES: My father often saw beyond the flesh.

KATE: Kissed such a creature!

HENRY: At such times she was beautiful.

KATE: [*with a touch of humility*] Yes, I'm sorry—I remember. Once I passed her, and instead of saying something, something horrible—she might—she looked down.

JOHN: She was beautiful, looking down.

KATE: [*angry*] And I, I suppose I wasn't beautiful to look at—

HENRY: No, I suppose not, that is, not for her.

KATE: [*viciously*] Well, let me tell you, you haven't inherited her beauty. Look at your hands—thick, hard, ugly—and the life lines in them like the life lines in the hands of every laborer digging sewers—

JOHN: There's something in that, but they are just beginning.

KATE: [*turning on them*] Look at you! You're ugly, and clumsy, and uncouth. You grunt and roar, you wear abominable clothes—and you have no manners—and all because of your father, your mighty righteous and original father. You don't have to be like this. You needn't have little pigs' eyes with bleached lashes, and thick hanging lips—and noses—but I suppose you've got adenoids, and you may suffer from the fact that your mother had a rupture, and in all probability you have the beginning of ulcers of the stomach, for God knows your father couldn't keep a meal down like a gentleman!

75

HENRY: He *was* delicate.

KATE: And why was he delicate? He called himself "The little Father," as one might say, "The great Emperor." Well, to have a father to whom you can go and say, "All is not as it should be"—that would have been everything. But what could you say to him, and what had he to say to you? Oh, we all have our pathetic moments of being at our best, but he wasn't satisfied with that, he wanted to be at it all the time. And the result, the life of a mole. "Listen and say nothing." Then he becomes the gentleman farmer because he discovers he cannot be the Beloved Fool. Suddenly he is the father of three creatures for all the world like Russian peasants—without an idea, a subtlety—it's wicked, that's all, wicked—and as for that, how do you know but that all three of you had a different mother? Why, great God, I might be the mother of one of you!

JOHN: [*significantly*] So I believe, madam.

KATE: [*unheeding*] Do you think a man like your father had any right to bring such children as you into the world—three columns of flesh without one of the five senses! [*She suddenly buries her head in her hands.*]

JOHN: [*gently*] You loved our father.

HENRY: And you also had your pot of honey—

KATE: Thank God I had no ideals—I had a religion.

JOHN: Just what?

KATE: You wouldn't understand.

HENRY: Shoes to the needy?

KATE: No, I'm not that kind, vicious boy.

JOHN: Are you quite certain?

KATE: I'll admit all my candles are not burning for God.

Well, then, blow them out, still I'll have a light burning somewhere, for all your great breaths, you oxen!

HENRY: You were never a tower builded of ivory—

KATE: You're too stupid to be bitter—your voices are too undeveloped—you'd say "love" and "hate" the same way.

JAMES: True, we have been shut away from intonations.

KATE: You wouldn't even wish to die.

JOHN: We shall learn.

KATE: Why bother?

JOHN: [*abruptly rising*] You have posed for the madonna?

KATE: Every woman has.

JOHN: You have done it better than most.

KATE: What do you mean?

JOHN: I looked at it when I came in. [*He picks up the photograph.*]

KATE: Let it be—I was playing in the "Crown of Thorns," an amateur theatrical.

JOHN: Yes, I presumed it was amateur—

JAMES: You were a devoted mother?

KATE: I have no virtues.

HENRY: And vices?

KATE: Weak in one, weak in the other.

JOHN: However, the baby had nice hands—

KATE: [*looking at him*] That is true.

JAMES: But then babies only use their hands to lift the breast, and occasionally to stroke the cheek—

KATE: Or throw them up in despair—not a heavy career.

JOHN: And then?

KATE: [*in an entirely new tone*] Won't you have tea?—

But no, pay no attention to me, that's another of my nasty malicious tricks. Curse life!

HENRY: Your life is drawing to a close.

JAMES: And from time to time you place your finger on a line of Nietzsche or Schopenhauer, wondering: "How did he say it all in two lines?" Eh?

KATE: As you say. [*She looks at them slowly, one by one.*] You are strange things. [*coming back*] But at least I've given up something—look at your mother, what did she give up for your father—a drunken husband—

JAMES: A drunken lover—that's different.

KATE: I can't help thinking of that great gross stomach of hers.

JAMES: Gross indeed, it won't trouble him any more.

KATE: What's that?

JOHN: He cut his throat with a knife—

KATE: Oh, my God! [*pause*] How did he look?

JOHN: You can't satisfy your aesthetic sense that way— he looked—well, ugly, played out; yes, played out. Everything had been too much for him—you—us— you could see that in the way he—

KATE: [*in a whisper*] Well, that's strange—everything seems—I knew him, you know. [*She begins to laugh.*] And the dogs barked?

JAMES: So I believe.

KATE: [*dazed*] And you, what are you three going to do?

HENRY: We are coming out of the country—we are going abroad—we can listen there.

KATE: Abroad—listen—what are you saying?

HENRY: There are great men abroad.

JAMES: Anatole France, De Gourmont—

KATE: De Gourmont is dead.

JOHN: There will be others.

KATE: [*still dully*] And how did you come to know such names—oh, your father, of course—

JOHN: We needed them.

KATE: Strange, I've been prepared for every hour but this—

JAMES: Yet I dare say you've never cried out.

KATE: You are mistaken. I've cried: "To the evil of mind all is evil—"

HENRY: Ah ha, and what happened?

KATE: Sometimes I found myself on my knees—

JAMES: And sometimes?

KATE: That's enough, haven't we about cleared all the shavings out of the carpenter shop?

HENRY: You at least will never kill yourself.

KATE: Not likely, I'll probably die in bed with my slippers on—you see, I have a pretty foot.

HENRY: We understand—you are about to be married.

KATE: To a supreme court judge—so I'm cleaning house.

JOHN: [*standing with the photograph*] But it won't be quite cleared out until this goes. [*He takes it out of the frame and turning it over reads.*] "Little John, God bless him." [*He turns it back.*] God bless him. Well, just for that I'd like to keep it.

KATE: That's my affair.

JOHN: So I see. [*He puts the photo in his blouse with the letters.*]

KATE: Well, perhaps—well, you're not so stupid after

all—Come, for the madonna give me back the letters—
I'll burn them, I swear, and you can put the madonna
at the foot of the bed.

JOHN: I shan't put it at the foot of the bed—I don't look
at the foot of the bed—

HENRY *and* JAMES: [*rising*] And now we shall go.

KATE: [*her hands to her head*] But, gentlemen, gentlemen—

HENRY: We won't need to bother you again. We are leaving the country and going elsewhere—and there was
only one of us to whom you might have shown a little
generosity—in other words we do not wish to be re-
minded, and now we can forget, and in time become
quite hilarious—

KATE: But, gentlemen, gentlemen, not this way—

JOHN: Well? [*Quite suddenly he takes her in his arms,
raises her face and kisses her on the mouth.*]

KATE: [*crying out*] Not that way! Not that way!

JAMES: That's the way you bore him!

[*The curtain drops behind them.*]

KURZY OF THE SEA

Kurzy of the Sea was first presented at the Province-town Playhouse in New York, March 26, 1920 with the following cast:

MOLLY MCRACE	Eda Heinemann
BETSY KEEP	Blanche Hays
PATRICK MCRACE	James Light
RORY MCRACE	Charles Ellis
KURZY	Norma Millay

Directed by Helen Westley.

Persons:
RORY MCRACE
MOLLY, his mother
PATRICK, his father
BETSY KEEP, a neighbor
KURZY, out of the sea

SCENE: *The McRace hut of turf, without window and with an earth floor. A settle covered with straw at left back used for bed and day seat. A square table near center with several three-legged stools standing about it. A large fireplace to left. Door at back leading out into the road.* RORY *is leaning against the jamb, smoking a pipe.*

RORY *is medium height, dark and possessed of a spirited melancholy.*

MOLLY MCRACE *is an astonishing portly and stately dame, much given to shawls and righteous indignation at the mention of "Free Will."*

BETSY KEEP *is an old woman, of the bent crooning but hardy style, keen of tongue and quick of mind. She is always "coming over" for the good of the "world."*

PATRICK MCRACE *is a sandy bearded man of fifty, with a long upper lip, a pride like the tides, and a huge liking for the women.*

KURZY *is small slender, handsome—saucy a little, and a little sad.*

MOLLY *and* BETSY *are seated at the table smoking pipes.* BETSY *is playing cards by herself.*

MOLLY: It's nothing I can be doing with him Betsy dear. Would you say, and you took a good look at him, that he is twenty-three years in the world and not enough down on him to stir in the wind? [*angrily shaking herself*] Ah heaven, it's all hot and suffering I am beneath my royal rags, thinking of the obstinacy of the boy, the downright damnedness of him.

BETSY: What's the matter with him?

MOLLY: Matter? It's plain impudent and unruly he is. It's often enough I've pleaded with him to get him a wife, it's not the rest of his life I can be cooking for him and his father feeding him, great stupid that he is. Well, if it's not married he is by sundown tomorrow, it's out of the house I'll be sending him, and no further ado.

BETSY: [*shuffling cards*] Has something got into him surely?

MOLLY: It's fairy tales has got him by the ear. Where does he be going at the full of the moon but to Black Peter's to hear his stories and his nonsense, and it's more than half daft he came into creation he was, what with crying out when he should be laughing, and laughing when he should be crying out, and him not three months old before he did be catching flies.

BETSY: First forward and then backward, eh?

MOLLY: Aye, it's crazy I am with him. May the curse be on Black Peter for what he's done to the mind of the lad, with his fairy tales.

BETSY: And how long is it since a fairy tale did be raking a man up so far he couldn't see a pretty pair of eyes or so in the whole world?

MOLLY: [*shifting back and forth*] Ah don't be asking me, who hasn't been able to sleep this twenty nights wondering what the world's coming to, with all its roads leading out over the earth, and Rory not taking one of them, and him doing nothing with his breath but drawing a pipe on it and making foolish promises what he'll consent to and what he won't, and him wearing out his Sunday breeches sitting on the rocks over the sea.

BETSY: Wasn't it married he ever wanted to be?

MOLLY: As it's plain to see, Betsy Keep, that it's not the worst you have been hearing. Well then, he says he'll marry quick enough and we give him a Queen or a Saint or a Venus, or whatever it is comes in with the tide.

BETSY: [*cackling to herself*] And what has he at all this side of his spine that would be drawing a Venus up out of the earth, or down out of the skies? If it's not a bit of barley he's stored away, or a pig or two for the smoking, there's not a Saint or a Venus at all, I'm thinking, will so much as put her nose over the blankets to make an eye at him.

RORY: [*taking his pipe out of his mouth for the fraction of a second*] Well then, why don't you be letting me alone?

MOLLY: [*turning toward* BETSY] It ain't as if I hadn't been honorable. I've bribed him, and with a right grand bribe at that. It's a fine shawl I have for his intended, and for himself I've offered the gray mare, and it the only thing we have in the world to prove to ourselves we are not dead surely, and done; for its four hoofs do be telling us, "You've a way to go yet before the end." But does it be making any difference? Sure it's old I am, and soon I'll have nothing to pledge but the stars and my great silence, but it's not Rory will mind his mother, but does be standing there, day after day, with never an intention in him.

BETSY: [*thumping her cane on the floor*] Rory, what's getting into you?

RORY: Nothing.

BETSY: Will you be answering me?

RORY: Nothing I'm saying, but if it's a wife I must get, why shouldn't I be picking and choosing, I'd be liking to know, and waiting a bit till the yellow hair of the world is brighter and longer, and the blue eyes bluer, before I'm taking a wife at all?

MOLLY: And who are you that can be giving the go-bye to the likes of Molly McGuire, and her the handsomest girl this side of the sea, and the light in her eyes will be the grief of God when they do be going out, and her famished for love of you.

RORY: She is not then, she's only playing with me, and trying to get me into trouble.

MOLLY: What do you mean?

RORY: She does be kicking me with her boot, and no one is looking.

BETSY: [*chuckling*] Ah, listen to the ignorance of him!

MOLLY: [*disgusted*] It's never a boot a woman does be shoving toward the kicking, but her heart is in it, Rory McRace, and you're a poor simpleton, and I doubt if you'll ever come into any kind of a mind at all.

BETSY: It's a deal of trouble you are Rory.

MOLLY: Aye, it's trouble he is, and his father out in the wind and the wet this many a night, setting traps and contrivances, and saying potions and prayers to the saints, trying to get so much as the tail of a goddess in his hand, one way or another, or the promise of a Venus, and him coming back exhausted surely, and soon the winter will be freezing his fingers so it's catching nothing he'll be, much less one of them fleeting spirits Rory's trembling for. Ah, it's my son is a drab thing and a slow.

RORY: [*grinning*] It's none so slow I am, I'm just a little aspiring.

MOLLY: [*fiercely*] If a Queen or a Goddess were brought to your very mouth, would you be accepting her?

RORY: [*comfortably*] I would that.

MOLLY: [*still more furious*] Even if she had broken a leg or so, and had torn her hair?

RORY: In any condition, providing she's a real unhuman woman.

At this moment there is a great noise and the voice of PAT MCRACE.

PAT: Open the door wider—I'm famished and can't hold her any longer.

MOLLY *darts to the door, admitting her husband who enters with a great fish net trailing behind him and in it what seems to be the figure of a woman, scantily draped, and very wet.*

MOLLY: By all the saints, Patrick McRace, what have you there?

PAT: Don't be asking fool questions, but fix the straw there, and give her a hand, can't you see she's fair logged?

They hurry to help lay her out in a comfortable position, flat on her back.

MOLLY: [*in an awed whisper*] And what is it at all, at all?
[*She crosses herself.*]

PAT: [*shaking the drops off his clothes, and wiping his
face with a red handkerchief, in a conceited voice*]
What does be coming in out of the belly of the sea,
into nets and the tide out, if it's not a spirit or a Venus
or whatever her name is, and it toward the darkness
of the night?

MOLLY: A real sea-going Venus?

PAT: The same. [*to his son*] Well here she is, be speaking
to her.

RORY: [*trembling*] She isn't real—I won't believe it, I
won't!

PAT: [*menacingly*] You won't believe it!

RORY: Did you *really* be dragging her in with the nets?

PAT: Did I be dragging her in with the nets? Well then,
be letting me tell you the astounding story of what Pat
McRace has done this day.

BETSY: Go on!

PAT: [*rubbing his hands*] Well then, I was sitting by the
edge of the water, where Lance keeps his boat bot-
tom-up, and the sea gulls were a-flying and a-flying,
and a-screaming and a-screaming on the very edges
of the waves themselves, and the stones near uncov-
ered from here to Kerry's Rocks, and the sea that dry
one would scorn to walk it. Well, I was mending my
nets, just sitting there and dangling my feet like, when
I see a strange thing, the strangest sight this side of
God—

MOLLY: Go on, go on!

PAT: [*complacently*] A man has to be getting a breath or

two when he's describing a woman. Well then, I was just watching the birds a-sitting and a-sitting and a-screaming and a-screaming and the waves lapping a bit and foaming, and then what should I see under my net, that was beginning to drag a bit in the tide, but a woman's face, with queer shut eyes and a satisfied look about the mouth. Says I to myself, by Gob, there's Rory's wife——and up I jumps, quick like, and gives the net a haul and another, and in she comes, as easy as you please, and not saying a word.

RORY: Ah, saints save us, it's a real spirit she is, and I'm lost!

PAT: [*unheeding*] As soon as I gets her in shore, I asks her what she was doing in the water, to make sure she was a mermaid or whatever it is that Rory wants, and if she had said that her lungs were fair cramped by the sea, or that she would be glad of a roll or two on her stomach, I would have shoved her back again and let her take care of herself. But she didn't, she just lay there staring up at the sun, a thing no human can do and not go blind or daft, and I was satisfied and took her up in my arms, and save for a few whispers like the sound in shells, she hasn't let a word out of her.

MOLLY: Did you be telling her the circumstances, and that she's to get the red shawl?

PAT: I made mention of it, kind of social like, but she didn't seem to notice. [*He pulls at his straps and stands regarding her.*] I suspect she's super-something, and so can't talk. [*continuing in a soft tone to himself*] It's a right tidy shape she has, and I'm beginning to respect my son for his love of the unnatural, for they don't be coming in and out of the world anywhere the likes of this I'm thinking—and though she has a look that's familiar—still she's right beautiful and uncanny.

RORY: [*approaching, frightened to death*] What's your name?

THE SEA-GOING GODDESS: Kurzy's me name, and good name it is, with a bite to it.

RORY: Is it a fancy you have taken to me Kurzy, and you just out of the deep?

KURZY: [*waving the question*] I got tired of seeing your mother, and her all dressed up, standing on the hill top, making incantations and signs, and you, going down into the bogs, with your fists clenched.

RORY: [*a little relieved*] Then it was spite, and not the strength of a great affection did be bringing you to the surface?

KURZY: [*radiantly*] It's spite that does be bringing a woman up through thirty fathoms of water, but it's love I'm thinking, does be driving her to shore.

MOLLY: [*throwing her arms about her son*] The Lord be thanked, for it's my prayers are answered, and now I'll be showing the young woman the shawl I have for her. [*She takes a bright red shawl down from a peg and approaches* KURZY.] Here you are darlint, and may you enjoy it hugely of evenings, when the dew is falling and there's no arms about your neck at all, at all.

KURZY: [*taking it*] Thank you kindly Ma'am.

RORY: [*looking about in an odd manner, and starting toward the door, knob in hand*] It's the gray mare I'll be getting—I'll be saddling her and taking my bride for a canter, will I da?

PAT: Ah sure, go ahead, if it's a spirit she is, it's no cold she'll be catching. [RORY *exits.*]

MOLLY: It's grand days we'll be having from now on, and Rory married and working at the keeping, for it's not a man in the world who can get him a wife, and then watch her go out in starvation surely.

PAT: And is it a grand bite to eat I do be getting for the deed I've done this day? [*He crosses and sits at the table.*]

MOLLY: It is Pat darlint, and as much as you will. [*She brings him bread, potatoes, etc.*] Ah Pat, I didn't like to be mentioning it, but it's a philosophy me old age has been bringing on, and it's not built to stand it I am. [*Through this speech there has been a dumb show of fear for* KURZY, *and a desire to propitiate her.* MOLLY *has given her a sup of tea, leaving the cup on the floor at a safe distance—and while talking all of them have not taken their eyes off her.*]

PAT: [*eating slowly*] What is it Molly dear?

RORY: [*in the door*] Come on Kurzy girl, I'll be riding into the dark with you, for the better whispering.

KURZY: [*who has tried to take a sup of tea, without succeeding*] Be carrying me then.

RORY: [*lifting her in his arms, and pausing in the door*] Perhaps it's soon I'll be back, and perhaps late. [*He goes out.*]

BETSY: Where do you suppose he'll be going, and why? [*She gets up and hobbles to the door.*]

PAT: Where and why do you suppose? To be making a little love before he does be settling down.

MOLLY: Which way does he be turning, Betsy?

BETSY: Toward the sea.

MOLLY: Toward the sea? [*pause*] It's grand fine she is Pat—

PAT: It's the sea water perhaps—who knows—

BETSY: She has a look to me—

MOLLY: I'm knowing what you would be saying—and I'm of the same mind—a too human look, eh Pat? But perhaps it'll wear off—

PAT: O aye.

MOLLY: Ah Pat, I wish we'd been saying the right thing in the world forever.

PAT: What is it now girl?

MOLLY: I was thinking, it's a hard word here, and a hard word there I've been putting past our Rory's ear, that he'll have difficulty forgetting perhaps, and perhaps not. [*She assumes a more cheerful air for no reason at all, excepting that she is Irish.*]

BETSY: [*swinging a little from side to side, in a monotonous crooning voice*] It's a long time we've been talking in the world for no good, but it's a longer we'll be silent for no good, it's for not good we come, and it's for no good we go, and there's no reason nor sense to our sorrow or our joy at all, but there's a little time left for a good long hugging of the fire, and a long sipping at the tea.

PAT: The pity of it, there's sense only to them as says there's none. It's right horrible discouraging they are.

MOLLY: [*cheerfully*] Sure, isn't it joy we do be getting this way or that? What does it matter if we do be getting it weeping or laughing? Ah sure, it's nothing can be covering up my head in darkness, now my son has got sense into him, and there's a woman in his life.

PAT: And now it's he will have to stop his dreaming and
his nonsense with a mighty stop. And it's he will have
to be turning a deaf ear on Black Peter when he does
be coming singing down out of the hills with the foolish eyes of him all lit up from below and shining, and
words coming out of him with a great rattle and a hurry
and a sorrow surely.

MOLLY: [*there's a silence, then in a quiet, thoughtful way*]
What way will we be knowing when the end is?
Another silence.

PAT: Hush! Did I hear horses hoofs—it's Rory coming
back I'm thinking.

RORY: [*striding into the room, hanging bridle up on a
peg on left wall*] I said I might be back quick.

PAT *and* MOLLY: What have you done?

RORY: I threw her back into the sea.

MOLLY *and* PAT: The prayers of the saints. [*They cross
themselves.*]

RORY: And I called out to her: "Kurzy girl, if you're a
saint it's I shall be knowing in a moment, for if you are
you'll swim, and if you're not, you'll drown—but in
either case, you can keep my mother's shawl."

MOLLY: Ah, Lord, Lord, and what did she say?

RORY: [*with a bit of pride*] It's a rare tongue has Kurzy,
and she calls out to me: "You're a dreamer Rory
McRace, or a fool, but in either case you can keep my
petticoat!"—and sure enough with that it came floating, and her in a neat little bathing suit like they keep
at Shannon's, and her white arms making for Kerry's
Rocks. "And take this back to your mother" she says.
"That it's often I've seen her standing on the hill making incantations for the fool she has for a son, but tell

her it's Pat McRace who has a bad memory for faces, for it's I am barmaid at the White Duck, and it's himself has dragged his nets through heavier stuff than water this many a night." And then she turned over on her back, and hanging onto the shawl, and begins floating, and added: "It's long distance swimming you'll be learning this summer, but it will do you little good," she says. "For by the time you can hold your own, I shall be halfway to Cork with a lover on my arm." And with that she turns over again and soon nothing could you see but the red of the shawl.

[*He walks to the door, looking back into the room.*] And you can be keeping your horse, mother, for it's a boat I shall be needing.

[curtain]

AN IRISH TRIANGLE

Playboy, No. 7, May 1921

An Irish Triangle was first presented at the Province-town Playhouse in New York, January 9, 1920, with the following cast:

KATHLEEN O'RUNE	Blanche Hays
SHIELA O'HARE	Leah Javne

Directed by Helen Westley.

Persons:
KATHLEEN O'RUNE, married
SHIELA O'HARE, unmarried

SCENE: *The interior of the O'Rune home. A neat little sitting room, with a high dresser, doors to right and left and a window at the back, overlooking a garden. A fireplace to left, with a pot on a hook. The table is set for tea, and the china and linen is of the best. Simple spotless curtains hang at the windows. The furniture is unobtrusive and arranged with an eye to effect.*

Little potted plants stand in a row on the sill, giving the room a feeling of warmth and color.

As the curtain rises KATHLEEN O'RUNE *is just shutting the door behind her friend* SHIELA O'HARE.

KATHLEEN O'RUNE *is a rather tall handsome woman. She wears a neat, almost stylish gown of blue and a saucy cap. Her general appearance is much above that of the usual poor.*

SHIELA O'HARE *is a middle aged woman, thin, small and sad.*

KATHLEEN: And how are you this fine day, Shiela, and the winter scarcely over and the spring coming?

SHIELA: It's grand, fine I am, and glad to see yourself my eyes have not been clapped on since last October, and me watching your man going down into the woods quiet like, and it the poaching season.

KATHLEEN: [*quite calmly*] It's a great change the world

has taken on since last it dropped down its leaves and the hares were running. And there's a rare mighty change come over things John does be putting his eyes on, for there's not a hare this side of the hills that doesn't be sitting tight on its tail and showing pleasure only, when John does be stepping down into the bogs.

SHIELA: Aye, its a stupendous change has come over nature, surely, since last May, Kathleen.

KATHLEEN: [*fussing with the tea things*] And will you be having a sup of tea? There's none better brewed from the Grace of God down [*pouring*] and will you be having sugar only, like the way your mother would be having it, and she lying on her back looking for the end?

SHIELA: I'll be having it so. You've a good memory Kathleen, though it is sealed up in silence and mystery you have been this six months. [*She pauses to look at* KATHLEEN, *over her tea cup.*]

KATHLEEN: [*pretending to notice nothing*] It's a surprising thing has been coming over me Shiela, this last six month, a fine thing and awesome thing surely for it's a look in on this poet and that I have, and it's a drop here and a bit there, I have learned of the nobility of literature, and an ear full of the subtleties of life you don't be hearing this side of the great doors of the Manor House.

At mention of the Manor house, SHIELA *chokes over her tea.*

KATHLEEN: [*going on*] Is the tea too strong for you Shiela dear? And you brewing it hours by the clock in your little hut by the road. Well, as I was saying, it's a look in on the tragedies of Russia and France and Spain I've been having this past season, and learning in how many styles one may lead a good life, though a hearty.

SHIELA: Is it books you have been reading?

KATHLEEN: It is then. It's licks and licks of grand stuff I have been memorizing to repeat to John when he does be coming in late—

SHIELA: [*off guard*] It's late I'm hearing he has been coming home since he saw the inside of the Manor door.

KATHLEEN: [*closing her eyes—*] Ah, it's late he is, but mighty keen to be hearing my fine voice dripping and riding over things with beauty in them like: "We must not think the Turk is so unskilled—" Or: "The heaving bosom holds an error hid—" How do you be liking it?

SHIELA: [*not liking it at all*] I do be liking it fine, but where did you be getting the taste?

KATHLEEN: [*rising*] And did you think, Shiela O'Hare, it was the rest of my life I was going to spend with my hands in my sleeve and my eyes on the churning only? Where would I be getting the taste? How would I know when to put my hair up and when to let it down? And how did I know these ferny plants were the right things and this perky cap that does be setting me like the sun on the hill top? And what of the lines of my dress that do be running down off my hips like they were going on until they discover the roots of elegance themselves? And where did I get the little lilt and catch in my voice, you might have been noticing, if you knew right from wrong, [*returning to her chair*] well, it's a long story and me not talking much.

SHIELA: [*coaxingly*] Ah, be telling me, and thereby lifting the tone of all Ireland.

KATHLEEN: Well, but wait a bit, 'till you be hearing me quote, for its quoting the likes of what I'll be telling you, that the gentry has risen from their knees and their prayers answered. Sure it's a risqué little piece from a Parisian journal I have for your ear now, but it smacks of what you don't know, so don't be surprised when the fine shivers of exaltation do be scampering down your spine.

SHIELA: [*excited*] Go on, go on!

KATHLEEN: Very well then, but be reminding me, when my eyes get that funny shiny, far away look, that I have a dressing gown and some under things I want to be showing you.

SHIELA: [*giggles nervously and takes another sup of tea*] I will then.

KATHLEEN: [*quoting*]

> Qui la, la jeune Fille
> He took her, il l'embrasse
> Miller, handsome Miller
> My collar you have torn
> Mon cap is chiffone
> Ah, la la!

SHIELA: [*tensely*] Sure it's like a grand lady you are acting this afternoon!

KATHLEEN: [*filling her cup*] It's not this afternoon alone that I do be acting the grand lady, but this many an afternoon, and my surroundings having difficulty to catch up to me at all, at all.

SHIELA: The sorrow has gone out of your eyes, and your

smile that used to be crooked with sadness, is glad and straight and does be "sassing" the sun.

KATHLEEN: [*bridling*] And next saying "whisht" to the sun when I'm caring. Ah, sure it's more like a peacock I am and me shaking my shoulders when I'm walking through the flowery ways of my garden only, and the birds singing of their high pleasure and the plow horses raising their hoofs and pausing a little before they be setting them back to earth again, and the bristles of heifers rolling from their throats down to their very tails with a shudder of joy for the song I do be making, and the spring coming.

SHIELA: It's a happy woman you are, but—

KATHLEEN: [*interrupting*] Sure it's a happy creature I am, and right proud of the glory and beauty of my limbs, and the independent ways of my breasts, and the little canny lights of my two eyes that do be striking fire and blazing this way and that. And it's John I'm better pleased with than any man in the country, for he's a good husband and a generous.

SHIELA: [*satisfied at last that the conversation has reached the point*] Aye, and how is John?

KATHLEEN: [*with perfect calm*] Right fine he is, and growing lean and losing the lines of the poacher and gaining the muscles of him, that do what he will, cannot trespass.

SHIELA: And what is he doing with himself these days— and nights? [*She is considerably frightened at her boldness, and dives into her cup.*]

KATHLEEN: Ah, it's the whole town is agog with it. And you yourself Shiela O'Hare haven't kept your tongue

quiet in your head, though it is a friend of mine you
have been since I was a child.

SHIELA: I never—

KATHLEEN: [*taking the words out of her mouth*] You
never set your foot out on the commons running past
the high Manor House, but you did be letting a whisper past you, or a deep sigh, or you would be casting
your eyes up in such a way as would put the whole
town a chattering and over-sugaring their tea. Ah, well,
it's I know the likes of you, but there's nothing in my
heart but that simple pity a fine woman feels for those
who have never seen the glory of the light.

SHIELA: [*unconvinced*] Aye?

KATHLEEN: Aye, it's months now a small smile has been
going about on the inside of my mouth for you all, and
for the things you would be "whisting" about and you
heard me coming, and the foolish look in the eye of
every married woman of you from here to Kildare—
wondering if my ways were her ways. But I'll be telling you, John is the envy of my heart and it's a great
thankfulness I have that I ever met him at all, and no
keening and swinging of the body this side and that,
because he has gone up on the hill and found her ladyship beautiful.

SHIELA: [*astounded, outraged*] If it were mine he was,
it's the good tuft of hair I would be wearing from his
left ear this night, and him traipsing about 'till moon
down, and the likes of you, standing in all your glory
waiting for the return of the whelp!

KATHLEEN: [*laughing*] Ah, it's mad you are, and it's a
sweet sight seeing you old women curling up at the

edges like dead leaves in the heat of the young fire is in my John.

SHIELA: If it's not your own honor you can be bitter enough to think of you might be thinking of the honor of other women with husbands who do be going to the fishing or the hunting, and they lying on their bellies among the fern and damp, or sweating over a sail that won't come down for the wet in it, and then them coming home with nothing about them to show for it but a long hair with a bit of curl in the end, that does be matching nothing in the house at all.

KATHLEEN: Sure, and it's a pity I have for all Ireland and them going about in the majority with no more sense than the likes of you Shiela O'Hare——with the bones of your body getting lighter and dryer day by day, waiting their turn in the grave, and never one of you hanging over the lips of him that's transgressed for the good that's in it.

SHIELA: [*tragically*] It's the curse is on you, for the way you do be talking and you a good woman.

KATHLEEN: Aye, it's a good woman I am but no fool. And where my man can go in body there I go in spirit, and if there's a better, more remembering, more observing man in the whole of the land than John O'Rune, I'd like to clap my eyes on him.

SHIELA: What will you be saying!

KATHLEEN: I'm saying: What he knows, I know, and what he sees, I see, and if there's anything her ladyship knows above me now, it's John has no words for the repeating. For there's nothing she says or does or thinks, but he does be telling me also, and she hasn't put a thing on her back this six months he hasn't described fine and it's the world will be seeing something this spring, I'm thinking, when I take my butter to market, for there's ways and ways of tying a ribbon, and there's ways and ways of greeting and farewelling, that the likes of us poor know nothing about at all, until we marry a lad with the sun in his hair, who is fit to nose it out at the end of a good love-making.

SHIELA: [*utterly mystified*] O aye?

KATHLEEN: Aye, it's few in the town will know how to wear a stocking as I shall wear mine, and there's few will know how to blow the nose with grandeur and with silence as I shall put into my linen from now on. And it's not a woman here nor there in the world at all who can be coming up to me and saying: "Kathleen O'Rune, they are wearing their hair simpler this season, and there's only two rows of lace to the under petticoat."

SHIELA: [*raising her hands*] That I should have lived to see this day!

KATHLEEN: "That you should have lived to see this day" [*with a grand gesture she sweeps the table clear of crumbs*] and you passing out of it no wiser, but it's I shall be swinging my hips with the grand swing, and it's I shall be rolling my eyes with a grand roll, and there'll be no one in the land so envious of me as you and your friends, who are afraid to do more than sit on the edges of their chairs when their husbands do be coming home late, with nothing to show for it, but a long hair with a bit of a curl to the end that does be matching nothing in the house at all.

SHIELA: [*sitting down again*] Where would the likes of the glory of Ireland and its women be if they were all as strange as yourself, Kathleen O'Rune, I'd like to know?

KATHLEEN: [*with a little impatience*] Well, I'll be telling you where you'd be. You'd be sitting among the hedges like the elves or the Queen, and knowing so much that you would be afraid to open your mouth for fear of confounding the priests themselves, who do be knowing a word or two of Greek and Latin and other Holy languages that no one has ever sinned in, and you would be having soft hands, and a nose could discriminate between the good clean smell of a man that has rolled in the grass, from that of pigs that do be snouting you out of bed in the dawn, and grunting around and making as much fuss as if you had borne them surely. And you'd be smiling with the straight smile that knows no sorrow, and the glint in your two eyes, and you would be lying down in the dark and rising up in the dawn with a sense in you that you had not stopped the great progress of the world by turning on your lean sides, dropping down tears, and lamenting out of your shallowness and your astounding ignorance. That's what you would be doing, and you had sense only.

SHIELA: [*taking up her shawl*] And is it the likes of this I must be spreading past the lintel, and you a woman I have loved since you were big enough to fall down.

KATHLEEN: It is then, and the sooner you can be spreading it the better, for it's in need of education is Ireland, and the refinement that comes down out of the hills, from behind grand doors, in the early dawn with red eyes.

SHIELA: Oh, ho!

KATHLEEN: And the only fear I have is that the women of the land will be outstripping the men, that's all. And now you may be going keening through the town of the things you have no part in, saying it's I have gone daft and right pleased at the change.

SHIELA: And it's I don't know what to make of you, and the terrible triangle that's come into your life! [*raising her head*]

KATHLEEN: It's the triangles that do be raising Ireland. [*She removes her cap.*] And it's the master of the Manor himself who is soft of tongue and charming, and John says there's a way he's dying to know, the master has of wrapping his puttees, that can be learned by close contact only.

SHIELA: It's blind mystified I am, and all turned about and mazed. [*She pauses shifting her shawl from one hand to the other. Then with sudden brightness*] You did be telling me to remind you there was a bit of underclothes you had, you would liking to show me—

KATHLEEN: Aye, I have—[*pause*]—it's a grand night coming on, and it's the moon and I will be climbing the hill, for I've nothing more to learn, but John is rare ignorant.

[*curtain*]

LITTLE DROPS OF RAIN

Wherein is Discussed the Advantage of xixth Century
Storm over xxth Century Sunshine

Vanity Fair, xix (September 1922)

An old and passionless garden, with clipped yew, clipped box, clipped arborvitae and a small clipped spaniel which runs around and around. The garden belongs to the American estates of the Anglo-American, MITZI TING. The garden is at once melancholy and charming, having some of the arboreal lèse-majesté of a wilderness and some of the hauteur of a well-groomed landscape.

LADY OLIVIA LOOKOVER is seated beside her niece, on a low marble bench. LADY LOOKOVER is a woman of seventy-six, of portly but coquettish mien; she wears a voluminous gown of pearl gray, with a fichu of black lace. Two small curls come down over her forehead, which is high, conical and surmounted by auburn tresses, done in Episcopal splendor in the shape of a miter.

MITZI TING is nineteen, fluffy and vivacious without quite knowing why. She is dressed in a simple little gown of white organdie, with bows down the back and ruffles up the front. She carries a pink parasol and regards her extremely small slippers fondly.

MITZI: [*pushing the ferrule of her parasol into the turf*] I know it's no longer done, Aunty, nevertheless, I have an irresistible desire to be driven down hill in a cab.

LADY LOOKOVER: [*with quiet sarcasm*] How wistful!

MITZI: You shall not make fun of me!

LADY LOOKOVER: My dear—fun?

MITZI: Yes, fun! I want to be driven down hill in a cab, any kind of cab, any kind of hill. How jolly it would be! The groom in red flannels, white trousers with black boots, and at my side a fellow versed in life, with a passion for pale ale, and a decided tendency to emulate the features of his favorite hound. You can see—

LADY LOOKOVER: I can see how utterly silly you are! In my day, the late XIXth century, it was quite the thing to do. In fact it is exactly what did happen. Never shall I forget that hour when, driving at breakneck speed, we, Sir Horace Droop (a few years my junior, it's true) and I, crossed the little bridge separating Uxbridge farm from Whitleys and turned into Lovers' Lane, only to have the rear axle give out. And there we sat, he toying with his cameo scarf pin, I with my mittens, and nothing on our stomachs but graham wafers.

MITZI: How sad!

LADY LOOKOVER: Not at all! How un-reproducible!

MITZI: Oh! I don't know, I have the same blood in my veins—

LADY LOOKOVER: Not at all. How can it be the same? In my day we had Beaconsfield and Beardsley, what have you? Barrie and Bennett. We were conceived in groups, you singly. Under the frock coat of your generation is but the torso of a gentleman; under the frills of the nineteenth century beats the heart of an indefatigable cynicism, made still sharper by a romantic twinge. You smile without satire; we curled the lip and Queens started up in bed. Your press is devoted to justice, I hear, but who leaves the door on the hasp? We whispered the word and the locks flew from the doors unbidden. We wept; you sigh. We died; you languish. Our wounds exposed the soul; yours can be covered by a single application of collodion. We believed in individual aristocracy; you in universal perturbation. We were the storm; you are the sunshine—

MITZI: Well, sunshine is very comfortable.

LADY LOOKOVER: Of course, that's the way you feel about it. You should. It's the way a puddle does feel about the sea. Now in my day we were different, because we were nearer the spinning wheel, the churn, the shuttle, the bodkin, the plow and the Tower of London. Our impulses were strong and our arteries not afraid of their function. As a consequence we were turbulent, boastful, enduring; you are anaemic, nervous. We had furies and killed; you have tantrums and retaliations. We rode to love and possibly to death when we went down hill in cabs. You would ride to safety and ennui.

MITZI: I don't admit all that. I have had advantages that you—

LADY LOOKOVER: Certainly, that's the point; if you always take advantage of your advantages they will demand the inevitable toll, which is less instinct and more education. My life was lived without punctuation, if I may use a comfortable figure of speech. Your life is riddled with colons and full stops.

MITZI: Well, what am I to do with my sense of romance?

LADY LOOKOVER: Don't over-estimate it, my dear. I am, as it were, the last leeway. You must conserve—

MITZI: I won't conserve. I want to abandon myself, to live fully—

LADY LOOKOVER: How spoiled you are!

MITZI: I'm not. Just because I'd rather have an interestingly warped life than a nicely rounded one; because I have an uncontrollable longing to go to the dogs—

LADY LOOKOVER: But you wouldn't have the faintest idea how to go to the dogs. On the other hand look at me. In my early youth I was called the ugliest woman on three continents. I was known everywhere as the Ugly Duck. I realized the value of that name. I made it my business to be a little more than ugly; it is that little extra that has made the world bow down since the first dawn. I was not only ugly, I was monstrous. Would you dare to be monstrous? No. I dared sun and rain, wind and hail, freckles and red nose. I was stout, I became gross; I was knock-kneed,—did I go in for calisthenics, as you would have been sure to do? No. I called it the Romantic Leg. Now no opera singer dares go on without it—

MITZI: [*awed*] You never took a mud bath, nor wore a mask?

LADY LOOKOVER: [*laughing a rich, rumbling laugh*] Mud bath! Mask! Would Napoleon have stopped crossing his hands behind his back for a million crowns? No. Ugliness and daring were my stock in trade, as his hands behind his back were his stock in trade.

MITZI: [*angrily*] Yet you were never married, you never finished your book on the "Correct Way to Hold the Snuff-box," you never had a child—

LADY LOOKOVER: [*wincing*] We won't discuss that.

MITZI: [*quickly*] Oh, I'm sorry! I didn't mean to hurt you, but you speak of Sir Horace Droop so often that I thought, well, perhaps, had all gone well—

LADY LOOKOVER: [*as if she had not been interrupted*] You, on the other hand, do not dare to be unattractive. You are pretty and passive and simpering. You have no temper and no virus. I had nothing to lose: therefore, I could afford to tear down the tapestries and return rings. That is the only kind of woman who should dare a hill.

MITZI: [*almost convinced*] Have I no future?

LADY LOOKOVER: [*almost gently*] Yes, but I am afraid that's all you have. We had a past, we were provided for, going and coming. I had Sir Horace Droop to play with; it's true I was a little old for him, but we got on. What have you? That self-made, clean-cut young fellow from Harvard to amuse you. What can you expect? I lived in a world bounded by heresy,——you in a garden sixty by sixty—

MITZI: It seems to me you are just a little too broad to suffer; suffering is a fine, fine point, and when it's very pointed it purifies.

LADY LOOKOVER: Who wants to be purified? I suffered gloriously, every fibre, every nerve, every pore winced with a high, magnificent torture. Purification would have been an intrusion!

MITZI: Everything you say makes me extremely miserable.

LADY LOOKOVER: [*closing her eyes*] When I was a girl I used to say to myself twice a day, once before my bath and once after: Olivia, react, it's the only way to keep above the people—we can't all have butlers you know.

MITZI: You are not a bit nice!

LADY LOOKOVER: Nice! And you want to drive down hill!

MITZI: I don't think that is so unreasonable, in spite of everything you said.

LADY LOOKOVER: Now don't excite yourself whatever you do!

MITZI: But I want to be eccentric—like you.

LADY LOOKOVER: [*pleased*] Why?

MITZI: Because I'll be seventy-six too, some day—

LADY LOOKOVER: [*wincing again*] You have to be born primed with eccentricity, otherwise accept oblivion!

MITZI: How extremely depressing you are.

LADY LOOKOVER: Of course, depression is a rule with me, you'll have to get used to it.

MITZI: Well, anyway suicide is open to me, and if I commit it in a nice risky way, you'll have to respect me—

LADY LOOKOVER: Nonsense! You are utterly unprovided for suicide. If you went up on the tower to do away with yourself, ten to one you would come down merely rumpled. You haven't the makings of a successful suicide—you lisp—

MITZI: [*trying in vain to control herself*] This is too much! Simply too much! What have you accomplished for all your seventy-six continental years? You are bankrupt, unmarried, childless—oh forgive me, I'm sorry! [LADY LOOKOVER *has put her handkerchief to her eyes*] but you drove me to it.

LADY LOOKOVER: [*closing and opening her eyes*

slowly] Ingrate! You are young, spoiled, pert! What do you know of my youth?

MITZI: [*hastily*] Nothing, nothing at all, excepting what you have told me, but I don't see why youth can't be exciting, in spite of the fact that I am perfectly safe from the Tower of London—

LADY LOOKOVER: [*indulgently*] You can be, and are, just little Anglo-American Mitzi Ting, nineteen and unnecessary. Expect nothing from your future but a respectable marriage to some nice, young business man who will drive you to church in a car, and who will kiss your hand with utter ignorance of the art of kissing.

MITZI: This is outrageous!

LADY LOOKOVER: My dear, accept the slowing down of the ages,—for you are, perhaps, one of its longest and most lingering notes.

MITZI: I can't stand this another instant! [*She starts up.*]

LADY LOOKOVER: Control, my dear, control—it's the best thing you Americans do! Your vitality is low. You mustn't do anything to shock it. You'll be sick.

MITZI: [*stamping her foot*] Lady Lookover, I am very fond of you, that is I was fond of you until a few moments ago. I have tried to respect your feelings and your age. I shall no longer do it. It is too much to expect. I wanted to spare you, but it is too late. I won't listen to another word! I, Mitzi Ting, American born, nineteen and lisping—was married to your Sir Horace Droop three perfect weeks ago today. Wait! Don't speak! [*She holds up a tiny and imperious pink palm.*] You may have been the Storm that wrecked him at the foot of the hill, but I was the Destiny after the Disaster. You were the Wind over the orchard of Love, perhaps, but I was the Lap into which he fell; that's what you must expect from the Languid. They are always left around after the Storm. Sir Horace Droop and I were thrown from our horses, while riding, instead of a cab, it's true, but as we sat in the dust of the bridle path, we looked at each other and realized that we could not have fallen in such perfect juxtaposition had we not been intended for one another. So! Adieu!

She flounces off, the parasol making a pink nimbus for her head, as LADY LOOKOVER *slowly raises her pince-nez to her nose.*

FIVE THOUSAND MILES

A Moral Homily Inspired by All the Current Talk about
the Wild Free Life in the South Seas

Vanity Fair, xx (March 1923)

The beach of a tropical island in the South Seas. It is high noon and excessively hot. The leaves of a single unknown plant wilt like the ears on a hundred hounds. There is no sound of insect or bird or reptile, no call of human voice, only the steady rhythmical lap of the sea.

Then, just as this loneliness and vastness is beginning to be amusing, a tiny speck is seen approaching from the left, a tinier speck approaching from the right. The specks continue for half an hour or so, and presently become man and maid, facing each other in this torrid noon.

He is very beautiful and rather bare; she is exquisite and no better off. A girdle, of almost reprehensibly sheer fern, encircles her waist. He wears a belt of riveted boar's tusks.

They are at a loss for an appropriate greeting.

SHE: Up la.

HE: Uggle uggle.

SHE: *Was willst du?*

HE: *Rien.*

SHE: Good Heaven!

HE: Thank God! [*They shake hands.*]

SHE: You are an American?

HE: And you, if I'm not mistaken, come from Virginia?

SHE: [*blushing beneath her tan*] How did you know?

HE: Your first sentence—Only a lady could have thought of it, a member of an old and honored family—

SHE: [*shuddering and turning pale beneath her tan*] Don't.

HE: Don't what?

SHE: Don't recall civilization to me. I came here, five thousand miles from everything, to forget convention and man-made law.

HE: That's odd, so did I. I came here, five thousand miles from anything I knew or loved or had acquired a habit for, just for those identical reasons.

SHE: Isn't it wonderful?

HE: Superb. But a little inaccessible. I've been here for five years.

SHE: [*starting*] Five years? Why, so have I. How did *you* get here?

HE: I got shipwrecked.

SHE: So did I.

HE: This is most strange.

SHE: [*an ugly light coming into her tender eyes*] Was it on the good ship *Nothingmore*?

HE: [*amazed*] It was.

SHE: [*covering her face with her hands*] Are you—Henry Allover?

HE: [*the light of recognition making his face radiant*] Is it possible that I am speaking to—to Mazie Notataul?

SHE: [*placing her open palms resignedly down upon her knees, which are now stretched out beneath the sun*] Well, it's inevitable, that's all. Here we are.

HE: [*awkwardly*] Yes, aren't we?

SHE: We might as well make it up.

HE: What?

SHE: Have you forgotten our quarrel?

HE: Oh of course; where were we, in the quarrel?

SHE: You had just broken away from your family, you had begun to doubt immortality. Don't you remember that, on the night of the storm on the ship *Nothingmore*, you asked me to take a turn with you about the deck? And then, suddenly you turned to me and said, in almost a religious voice "I believe in nature. I hate conventionality. I am flying from it."

HE: Did I?

SHE: You did. The implication of your simple words almost carried me away. Then you said that love should be like that. That you would have, for your mate, no one who did not believe in Nature. And then you said that any girl you loved must be the kind who thought nothing of convention, who lived a free untutored life.

HE: Ah, yes, to be sure, I remember—

SHE: Well, I agreed with you, in everything you said.

HE: Really?

SHE: Well, aren't you going to make any deductions.

HE: [*trying*] I deduce that, once here, five thousand miles from civilization, you determined to live your life, freely, beautifully—

SHE: [*temporarily off her guard*] Yes, and with no thought of consequences.

HE: [*impulsively*] Wonderful, gorgeous, courageous woman!

SHE: And you?

HE: Since I have been here, five thousand miles from civilization, I have been trying to forget you. I thought of course that you would marry that captain from West Point.

SHE: And we've been within a stone's throw from each other, here, on this tropical island for five years and never met before.

HE: I seldom come up to this part of the beach.

SHE: I seldom leave it—but we have found each other at last.

HE: Yes, haven't we?

SHE: Well, and now what?

HE: I don't know.

SHE: Do you still love me?

HE: I adore you—

SHE: Well?

HE: That's all. That's a simple feeling, simply stated.

SHE: [*impatiently*] Is idiocy one of the requisites of simplicity?

HE: What do you mean?

SHE: For Heaven's sake, kiss me!

HE: [*putting an arm about her and kissing her*] Are you— are you—mine?

SHE: Entirely. As you wanted me to be, five years ago. Simple, untouched by convention, daring all civilizations, and the savagery we are living in. Five thousand miles from anywhere, willing to face any kind of criticism—yours, before Heaven. [*They are standing now and kiss each other with a passion and fervor that makes the boar's tusks rattle. Suddenly, with a little scream—the moon having broken roughly through the clouds—she says:*] My God, what's that?

HE: What's what?

SHE: That, there—on the sand, it came in with the last wave! It's—a—it's a— [*She frees her waist of his arms while her manner changes to one of congealed hauteur.*] We are followed. A ship must be nearing the island. People! Your family, or mine! You must leave me—at once. [*She draws her ferns about her.*] It's no use, Henry Allover, we can't get away from society.

HE: [*dumbfounded, peering down at an object on the sand*] What *is* it?

SHE: [*in a stark whisper*] An egg-beater!

TWO LADIES TAKE TEA

Shadowland, VII (April 1923)

The drawing-room of COUNTESS NICOLETTA
LUPA'S *little villa overlooking one of the bluest of Italian lakes.*

The walls are sweetly melancholy with prints of a past voluptuousness. A myriad of tiny glass pendants impale the atmosphere on their darting points. Venetian mirrors, that lied with brittle persistence in an age long past, still lie, but the task is not an ungracious one, for the face that pauses before them occasionally, is at once enigmatic, handsome and daring.

The COUNTESS *is seated at a desk, resting the hilt of a pearl-handled pen lightly against her cheek. Though seated, it is evident that she is tall and stately. She is miraculous with black lace, and pernicious with unpurchasable perfume. The motif of her blue and red earrings is carried out by the tall windows directly behind her, representing the Nativity at that moment when the Mother is most poignantly convalescent.*

The COUNTESS *is of uncertain years. When she moves it is with a dangerous smallness of gesture, the movement of a sword in a scabbard, accompanied by just the right murmur of rebellious ribbons and desperate taffeta. She is so fearfully blasé that she does not care where her next shudder is coming from.*

She is alone, though she is evidently expecting a single person to tea. Two delicate cups stand upon a tray near at hand.

The sound of a distant bell is heard, and somewhere from the lake the cry of a grieving bird, just deciding to stand on both feet.

There then descends silence. Presently, however, the COUNTESS *is aware of the presence of* FANNY BLAZE, *a young American. She has come along the garden path, and now, stands leaning against the casement. Slowly she comes in. She is blonde, dressed in hyacinth, and is without ornament save for a single red rose, which she has placed behind her ear. When in Italy do as the Italians, etc.*

She is below medium in height, but as one might say, exquisitely lacking in inches. It is evident that the two have met both for tea and for no good.

FANNY: [*coming forward, directly, warmly*] May I?

LUPA: [*rising, gracious, both hands extended*] Oh, my dear!

FANNY: It is very warm, isn't it?

LUPA: Detestable! But here, in the shade—

FANNY: Perfect.

LUPA: [*pouring tea*] Perhaps you would rather have something with ice in it?

FANNY: Oh I thank you, no. Just a little lemon. It's always so touching to be Russian in Italy.

LUPA: [*the shade of a smile hovering over her lips*] Or at home abroad—or calm during a storm—

FANNY: [*moving her spoon in a perfect circle*] Quite.

LUPA: [*softly, in a voice pitched to hospitality*] You are in love with my husband, the Count?

FANNY: [*turning her head a little to one side, arranging the rose*] Ravished.

LUPA: Is it possible that you are naïve?

FANNY: No, brilliant.

LUPA: I see. Well, as my husband's wife, what have you to offer?

FANNY: Nothing. He is bound to accept.

LUPA: Are you—rich?

FANNY: But not quite American

LUPA: I love little, blonde, frank women.

FANNY: And I, I am fascinated by your tall brutality.

LUPA: Of course, you know that I ride better than you?

FANNY: Undoubtedly

LUPA: I have my own way with animals.

FANNY: [*enthusiastically*] Don't I know it.

LUPA: [*drawling sightly*] I have a beautiful foot. It looks well in a stirrup, descending a staircase, on a neck—

FANNY: [*nodding*] While mine are deformed with pinching. But they are piquant—

LUPA: And I have a sharp tongue—

FANNY: My dear Countess, you are brilliant, adorable, fascinating! Were I a man I would choose you, of course. But men are fools, they adore safety; therefore your husband will follow me home like a chick.

LUPA: [*leaning forward on one ringed hand*] Just what does he see in you?

FANNY: Well, to put it in the Scott Fitzgerald way: the speechless and dumbfounded.

LUPA: Let us put it still another way: What is wrong with me?

FANNY: [*impatiently*] You are superb. That is enough. If we were liqueur I could explain it even better, by saying that I am moonshine and you are aged in the wood. You are too perfect. You need no pruning. What possible use have you for a lifelong devotion? You will continue, like the sea, no matter what little sloops are set upon you.

LUPA: [*smiling*] What will you do with Nicoletti when you get him?

FANNY: Heavens! I hadn't thought of that. [*She begins counting off on her fingers.*] I promise to muffle him against the cold, to introduce him to at least one new dish a season, and once in a long while I shall make him a trifle jealous, as we sit in the first-class carriage of some train, leaving one place for another.

LUPA: You almost convince me—

FANNY: [*with a sigh of ecstasy*] Darling!

LUPA: [*rising to her full height, lighting a cigarette with fearful poise*] You see, to begin with, the Count has one of those debauched skulls that come to a family only when the blood can feel no more terror, the heart no more anguish and the mind no further philosophy. The Count is built in every line for a magnificent funeral—neither more nor less. It will be his last gesture. [*raising her hand*] Wait, I'm not proposing to kill him. He'll do it all in good time, at just the right moment, perfectly, leisurely. It will, I promise you, be superb, irrevocably complete. It will however, as I said, be his last, his very last gesture, my dear Fanny Blaze.

FANNY: [*rising nervously*] I've only your word for it.

LUPA: [*laughing, a soft mirthless laugh*] My word, my dear? No, you have the assurance of the ages. Look at him for yourself. What you took for princeliness and grandeur was princely and was grand, but the princeliness came from the knowledge that after me there will be no one; and the grandeur from the security of such a knowledge. The Count was tired when I married him, some twenty-odd years ago. [*holding out her hand with a generous movement, not unalloyed with amusement*] On my word of honor, my dear—

FANNY: Somehow—I feel—extremely ridiculous, all of a sudden—it was so nice before—

LUPA: And will be again. You must not despair; you are a young and charming girl, and you have one priceless quality—it's bound to take you far—

FANNY: What?

LUPA: That "See her first" impulse, very rare my dear, very rare.

FANNY: You are making fun of me.

LUPA: No, I'm putting you where you belong.

FANNY: Countess Lupa!

LUPA: [*disregarding the interruption*] Ahead of your time; you were just a little inclined toward the wrong generation, that's all.

FANNY: What do you mean?

LUPA: That your future is assured, my dear. I have a son.

TO THE DOGS

First published in *A Night Among the Horses*
(New York: Horace Liveright, 1929).

Persons:

HELENA HUCKSTEPPE

GHEID STORM, her neighbor

Time:

Late afternoon.

Place:

In the mountains of Cornwall-on-Hudson—the Hucksteppe house.

SCENE: *The inner room of the Hucksteppe cottage.*

To the left, in the back wall, a large window overlooks a garden. Right center, a door leads off into a bedroom, and from the bedroom one may see the woods of the mountain. The door is slightly open, showing a glimpse of a tall mirror and the polished pole of a bed.

In the right wall there is a fireplace.

A dog lies across the threshold, asleep, head on paws.

About this room there is perhaps just a little too much of a certain kind of frail beauty of object. Crystal glasses, scent bottles, bowls of an almost too perfect design, furniture that is too antiquely beautiful.

HELENA HUCKSTEPPE, *a woman of about thirty-five, stands almost back view to the audience, one arm lying along the mantel. She is rather under medium in height. Her hair, which is dark and curling, is done carefully about a small fine head. She is dressed in a dark, long gown, a gown almost too faithful to the singular sadness of her body.*

At about the same moment as the curtain's rising, GHEID STORM *vaults the window sill. He is a man of few years, a well-to-do man of property, brought up very carefully by upright women, the son of a conscientious physician, the kind of man who commutes with an almost religious fervor, and who keeps his wife and his lawns in the best possible trim, without any particular personal pleasure.*

GHEID is tall, but much too honorable to be jaunty, he is decidedly masculine. He walks deliberately, getting all the use possible out of his boot-leather, his belt-strap and hat-bands.

His face is one of those which, for fear of misuse, has not been used at all.

HELENA HUCKSTEPPE does not appear to be in the least astonished at his mode of entrance.

GHEID STORM: As you never let me in at the door, I thought of the window. [HELENA *remains silent.*] I hope I did not startle you. [*pause*] Women are better calm, that is, some kinds of calm—

HELENA: Yes?

STORM: [*noticing the dog, which has not stirred*] You've got funny dogs, they don't even bark. [*pause*] I expected you'd set them on me; however, perhaps that will come later—

HELENA: Perhaps.

STORM: Are you always going to treat me like this? For days I've watched you walking with your dogs of an evening—that little black bullpup, and then those three setters—you've fine ways with you, Helena Hucksteppe, though there are many tales of how you came by them—

HELENA: Yes?

STORM: Yes. [*pause*] You know, you surprise me.

HELENA: Why? Because I do not set my dogs on you?

STORM: Something like that.

HELENA: I respect my dogs.

STORM: What does that mean?

HELENA: Had I a daughter, would I set her on every man?

STORM: [*trying to laugh*] That's meant for an insult, isn't it? Well, I like the little insulting women—

HELENA: You are a man of taste.

STORM: I respect you.

HELENA: What kind of a feeling is that?

STORM: A gentleman's—

HELENA: I see.

STORM: People say of you: "She has a great many ways—"

HELENA: Yes?

STORM: [*sitting on the edge of the table*] "But none of them simple."

HELENA: Do they?

STORM: [*without attempting to hide his admiration*] I've watched your back: "There goes a fine woman, a fine silent woman; she wears long skirts, but she knows how to move her feet without kicking up a dust—a woman who can do that, drives a man mad." In town there's a story that you come through once every spring, driving a different man ahead of you with a riding whip; another has it, that you come in the night—

HELENA: In other words, the starved women of the town are beginning to eat.

STORM: [*pause*] Well [*laughs*] I like you.

HELENA: I do not enjoy the spectacle of men ascending.

STORM: What are you trying to say?

137

HELENA: I'm saying it.

STORM: [*after an awkward pause*] Do—you wish me to—go away?

HELENA: You will go.

STORM: Why won't you let me talk to you?

HELENA: Any man may accomplish anything he's capable of.

STORM: Do you know how I feel about you?

HELENA: Perfectly.

STORM: I have heard many things about your—your past— I believe none of them—

HELENA: Quite right, why should you mix trades?

STORM: What do you mean by that?

HELENA: Why confuse incapability with accomplishment—

STORM: It's strange to see a woman like you turning to the merely bitter—

HELENA: I began beyond bitterness.

STORM: Why do you treat me this way?

HELENA: How would you have me treat you?

STORM: There was one night when you seemed to know, have you forgotten? A storm was coming up, the clouds were rolling overhead—and you, you yourself started it. You kissed me.

HELENA: You say it was about to storm?

STORM: Yes.

HELENA: It even looked like rain?

STORM: Yes.

HELENA: [*quickly, in a different voice*] It was a dark night, and I ended it.

STORM: What have I done?

HELENA: You have neglected to make any beginning in the world—can I help that?

STORM: I offer you a clean heart.

HELENA: Things which have known only one state, do not interest me.

STORM: Helena!

HELENA: Gheid Storm.

STORM: I have a son; I don't know why I should tell you about him, perhaps because I want to prove that I have lived, and perhaps not. My son is a child, I am a man of few years and my son is like what I was at his age. He is thin, I was thin; he is quiet, I was quiet; he has delicate flesh, and I had also—well, then his mother died—

HELENA: The saddle comes down from the horse.

STORM: Well, she died—

HELENA: And that's over.

STORM: Well, there it is, I have a son—

HELENA: And that's not over. Do you resent that?

STORM: I don't know, perhaps. Sometimes I say to myself when I'm sitting by the fire alone— "You should have something to think of while sitting here"—

HELENA: In other words, you're living for the sake of your fire.

STORM: [*to himself*] Some day I shall be glad I knew you.

HELENA: You go rather fast.

STORM: Yes, I shall have you to think of.

HELENA: When the fire is hot, you'll be glad to think of me?

STORM: Yes, all of us like to have a few things to tell to

our children, and I have always shown all that's in my heart to my son.

HELENA: How horrible!

STORM: [*startled*] Why?

HELENA: Would you show everything that made your heart?

STORM: I believe in frankness—

HELENA: [*with something like anger*] Well, some day your son will blow his head off, to be rid of frankness, before his skin is tough.

STORM: You are not making anything easier.

HELENA: I've never been callous enough to make things easier.

STORM: You're a queer woman—

HELENA: Yes, that does describe me.

STORM: [*taking his leg off the table*] Do you really want to know why I came? Because I need you—

HELENA: I'm not interested in corruption for the many.

STORM: [*starting as if he had been struck*] By God!

HELENA: Nor in misplaced satisfactions—

STORM: By God, what a woman!

HELENA: Nor do I participate in liberations—

STORM: [*in a low voice*] I could hate you!

HELENA: I limit no man, feel what you can.

STORM: [*taking a step toward her, the dog lifts its head*] If it were not for those damned dogs of yours—I'd—I'd—

HELENA: Aristocracy of movement never made a dog bite—

STORM: That's a—strange thing to say—just at this moment.

HELENA: Not for me.

STORM: [*sulky*] Well, anyway, a cat may look at a King—

HELENA: Oh, no, a cat may only look at what it sees.

STORM: Helena Hucksteppe.

HELENA: Yes.

STORM: I'm—attracted—to you.

HELENA: A magnet does not attract shavings.

STORM: [*with positive conviction*] I *could* hate you.

HELENA: I choose my enemies.

STORM: [*without warning, seizing her*] By God, at least I can kiss you! [*He kisses her full on the mouth—she makes no resistance.*]

HELENA: [*in a calm voice*] And this, I suppose, is what you call the "great moment of human contact."

STORM: [*dropping his arms—turning pale*] What are you trying to do to me?

HELENA: I'm doing it.

STORM: [*to himself*] Yet it was you that I wanted—

HELENA: Mongrels may not dig up buried treasure.

STORM: [*in a sudden rage*] You can bury your past as deep as you like, but carrion will out!

HELENA: [*softly*] And this is love.

STORM: [*his head in his arms*] Oh, God, God!

HELENA: And you who like the taste of new things, come to me?

STORM: [*in a lost voice*] Shall I have no joy?

HELENA: Joy? Oh, yes, of a kind.

STORM: And you—are angry with me?

HELENA: In the study of science, is the scientist angry when the fly possesses no amusing phenomena?

STORM: I wanted—to know—you—

HELENA: I am conscious of your failure.

STORM: I wanted something—some sign—

HELENA: Must I, who have spent my whole life in being myself, go out of my way to change some look in you?

STORM: That's why you are so terrible, you have spent all your life on yourself.

HELENA: Yes, men do resent that in women.

STORM: Yes, I suppose so. [*pause*] I should have liked to talk of—myself—

HELENA: You see I could not listen.

STORM: You are—intolerant.

HELENA: No—occupied—

STORM: You are probably—playing a game.

HELENA: [*with a gracious smile*] You will get some personal good out of it, won't you?

STORM: I'm uncomfortable—

HELENA: Uncomfortable!

STORM: [*beginning to be really uncomfortable*] Who *are* you?

HELENA: I am a woman, Gheid Storm, who is *not* in need.

STORM: You're horrible!

HELENA: Yes, that too.

STORM: But somewhere you're vulnerable.

HELENA: Perhaps.

STORM: Only I don't quite know the spot.

HELENA: Spot?

STORM: Something, somewhere, hidden—

HELENA: Hidden! [*She laughs.*] *All* of me vulnerable.

STORM: [*setting his teeth*] You tempt me.

HELENA: [*wearily*] It's not that kind.

STORM: I've lain awake thinking of you—many nights.

HELENA: That is too bad.

STORM: What is too bad?

HELENA: That you have had—fancies.

STORM: Why?

HELENA: Theft of much, makes much to return—

STORM: The world allows a man his own thoughts.

HELENA: Oh, no—

STORM: At least my thoughts are my own.

HELENA: Not one, so far.

STORM: What does that mean?

HELENA: You'll know when you try to think them again.

STORM: You mean I'm not making headway—well, you're right, I'm not—

HELENA: Now tell me what brought you through the window.

STORM: [*relieved*] I'm glad you ask that, it's the first human thing that's happened this afternoon.

HELENA: You have forgotten our great moment of human contact.

STORM: [*nervously*] Well—

HELENA: You were about to tell me what brought you?

STORM: I don't know—something no one speaks of— some great ease in your back—the look of a great lover—

HELENA: So—you scented a great lover—

STORM: I am a man—and I love—

HELENA: What have you done for love, Gheid Storm?

STORM: I've—never gone to the dogs—

HELENA: So?

STORM: I've always respected women.

HELENA: In other words: taken the coals out of the fire with the poker—continue—

STORM: That's all.

HELENA: And you dared to come to me! [*Her entire manner has changed.*]

STORM: No matter what you've been—done—I love you.

HELENA: Do not come so near. Only those who have helped to make such death as mine may go a little way toward the ardors of that decay.

STORM: What have I done?

HELENA: You have dared to bring to a woman, who has known love, the whinny of a pauper.

STORM: What am I?

HELENA: [*softly, to herself*] How sensitively the handles cling to the vase, how delicate is the flesh between the fingers.

STORM: I—I don't know you.

HELENA: [*dropping her hands to her sides*] Come here, Gheid Storm—[GHEID *approaches slowly, like a sleep walker.*] Put your hand on me. [*He does so as if in a dream.*] So! [*She looks first at his hand, then into his face, making it quite plain that he does not even know how to touch a woman.*] Yet you would be my lover, knowing not one touch that is mine, nor one word that is mine. My house is for men who have done their stumbling.

STORM: [*in an inaudible voice*] I am going now—

HELENA: I cannot touch new things, nor see beginnings.

STORM: Helena! Helena!

HELENA: Do not call my name. There are too many names that must be called before mine.

STORM: Shall I die, and never have known you?

HELENA: Death, for you, will begin where my cradle started rocking—

STORM: Shall I have no love like yours?

HELENA: When I am an old woman, thinking of other things, you will, perhaps be kissing a woman like me—

STORM: [*moving blindly toward the door*] Now I am going.

HELENA: [*in a quiet, level voice*] The fall is almost here.

STORM: Yes, it's almost here.

HELENA: The leaves on the mountain road are turning yellow.

STORM: Yes, the leaves are turning.

HELENA: It's late, your son will be waiting dinner for you.

STORM: Don't take everything away.

HELENA: You will not even recall having seen me.

STORM: Can memory be taken too?

HELENA: Only that memory that goes past recollection may be kept.

STORM: [*at the door*] Good night—

HELENA: [*smiling*] There is the window.

STORM: I could not lift my legs now.

HELENA: That's a memory you may keep.

STORM: Good night.

HELENA: Goodby, Gheid Storm, and as you go down the hill, will you lock the gate, a dog thief passed in the night, taking my terrier with him.

STORM: The one with the brown spots?

HELENA: Yes.

STORM: That was a fine dog.

HELENA: Yes, she was a fine dog—restless.

STORM: They say any dog will follow any man who carries aniseed.

HELENA: Well, soon I return to the city.

STORM: You look tired.

HELENA: Yes, I am tired.

> GHEID *exits.* HELENA *takes her old position, her back almost square to the audience.*
>
> [*curtain*]

THE DOVE

First published in *A Night Among the Horses*
(New York: Horace Liveright, 1929).

First presented at the Studio Theatre, Smith College, 1926.

Also presented at Bayes Theatre, New York City

Persons:

AMELIA BURGSON and VERA BURGSON, sisters
THE DOVE, A young girl living with the BURGSONS
TIME: Early morning.
PLACE: The Burgson apartment, a long, low rambling affair at the top of a house in the heart of the city.

The decoration is garish, dealing heavily in reds and pinks. There is an evident attempt to make the place look luxuriously sensual. The furniture is all of the reclining type.

The walls are covered with a striped paper in red and white. Only two pictures are evident, one of the Madonna and child, and one of an early English tandem race.

There are firearms everywhere. Many groups of swords, ancient and modern, are secured to the walls. A pistol or two lie in chairs, etc.

There is only one door, which leads out into the back hall directly back center.

AMELIA BURGSON *is a woman rather over the normal in height, with large braids of very yellow hair, done about a long face. She seems vitally hysterical.*

VERA BURGSON *is small, thin and dark.*

THE DOVE *is a slight girl barely out of her teens; she is as delicate as china with almost dangerously transparent skin. Her nose is highbridged and thin, her hands and feet are also very long and delicate. She has red hair, very elegantly coiffured. When she moves (seldom) the slightest line runs between her legs, giving her the expectant waiting air of a deer.*

At the rising of the curtain THE DOVE, *gowned in white, is seated on the divan polishing the blade of an immense sword. Half reclining to her right lies* VERA *in a thin yellow morning gown. A French novel has half fallen from her hand. Her eyes are closed.*

THE DOVE: Yes, I'm hurrying.

VERA: That's best, she will be back soon.

THE DOVE: She is never gone long.

VERA: No, never very long—one would grow old waiting for the day on which she would stay an hour—a whole hour.

THE DOVE: Yes, that's true.

VERA: [*wearily*] She says we live dangerously; [*laughs*] why, we can't even keep the flies out.

THE DOVE: Yes, there are a great many flies.

VERA: [*after a pause*] Shall I ever have a lover, do you suppose?

THE DOVE: [*turning the sword over*] No, I suppose not.

VERA: Yet Amelia and I have made it our business to know—everything.

THE DOVE: Yes?

VERA: Yes. We say this little thing in French and that little thing in Spanish, and we collect knives and pistols, but we only shoot our buttons off with the guns and cut our darning cotton with the knives, and we'll never, never be perverse though our entire education has been about knees and garters and pinches on hind-quarters—elegantly bestowed—, and we keep a few animals—very badly—hoping to see something first-hand—and our beds are as full of yellow pages

and French jokes as a bird's nest is full of feathers—
God! [*she stands up abruptly*] little one, why do I wear
lace at my elbows?

THE DOVE: You have pretty arms.

VERA: Nonsense! Lace swinging back and forth like that,
tickling my arms, well, that's not beauty—

THE DOVE: I know.

VERA: [*returning to her couch*] I sometimes wonder what
you do know, you are such a strange happening, anyway. Well then, tell me what you think of me and what
you think of my sister, you have been here long enough.
Why do you stay? Do you love us?

THE DOVE: I love something that you have.

VERA: What?

THE DOVE: Your religious natures.

VERA: Good heavens!

THE DOVE: You misunderstand me. I call that imagination that is the growth of ignorance, religion.

VERA: And why do you like that?

THE DOVE: Because it goes farther than knowledge.

VERA: You know, sometimes I wish—

THE DOVE: Yes?

VERA: That you had lived all we pretend we have.

THE DOVE: Why?

VERA: I don't know, but somehow some one like you
should know—everything.

THE DOVE: Do I seem so young?

VERA: I know, that's what's so odd. [*impatiently*] For
heaven's sake, will you stop polishing that infernal
weapon!

THE DOVE: [*quietly*] She said to me: "Take all the blood stains off first, then polish it."

VERA: There you are; she is quite mad, there's no doubt. Blood stains! Why, she would be afraid to cut her chops with it—and as for the rest of her manifestations— nonsense!

THE DOVE: She carries a pistol with her, just to go around the corner for a pound of butter.

VERA: It's wicked! She keeps an enormous blunderbuss in the corner of her room, but when I make up her bed, all I find is some Parisienne bathing girl's picture stuck full of pin holes—

THE DOVE: I know, she sits beside me for hours making those pin holes in the borders of everything in sight.

VERA: [*with a strange anger*] Why do you stay?

THE DOVE: Why should I go?

VERA: I should think this house and two such advanced virgins as Amelia and myself would drive you to despair—

THE DOVE: No, no, I'm not driven to despair—

VERA: What do you find here?

THE DOVE: I love Amelia.

VERA: Another reason for going away.

THE DOVE: Is it?

VERA: Yes, it is.

THE DOVE: Strange, I don't feel that way about it.

VERA: Sometimes I think—

THE DOVE: Yes?

VERA: That you are the mad one, and that we are just eccentric.

THE DOVE: Yet my story is quite simple.

VERA: I'm not so certain.

THE DOVE: Yet you have heard it.

VERA: There's more than one hears.

THE DOVE: I was born on a farm.

VERA: So you say.

THE DOVE: I became very fond of moles—it's so daring of them to be in the darkness underground. And then I like the open fields, too—they say there's nothing like nature for the simple spirit.

VERA: Yes, and I've long had my suspicions of nature.

THE DOVE: Be that as it may, my brothers were fond of me—in a way, and my father in—a way—then I came to New York—

VERA: And took up the painting of china—

THE DOVE: Exactly. I was at that for three years, then one day I met you walking through the park, do you remember? You had a parasol, you tipped it back of your head, you looked at me a long time. Then I met Amelia, by the same high fence in the same park, and I bowed to her in an almost military fashion, my heels close together—

VERA: And you never did anything wild, insane—

THE DOVE: It depends on what you call wild, insane—

VERA: [*with great excitement*] Have you ever taken opium or hashish?

THE DOVE: [*as if answering*] There are many kinds of dreams—in one you laugh, in another you weep—

VERA: [*wringing her hands*] Yes, yes, once I dreamed. A dream in the day, with my eyes wide open. I dreamt I was a Dresden doll and that I had been blown down by the wind and that I broke all to pieces—that is, my arms and my head broke all to pieces—but that I was surprised to find that my china skirt had become flexible, as if it were made of chiffon and lace.

THE DOVE: You see, there are many dreams—

VERA: Have you ever felt that your bones were utterly sophisticated but that your flesh was keeping them from expressing themselves?

THE DOVE: Or vice versa?

VERA: Yes, or vice versa.

THE DOVE: There are many kinds of dreams—

VERA: You know, I'm afraid of you!

THE DOVE: Me?

VERA: Yes, you seem so gentle—do we not call you the Dove? And you are so little—so little it's almost immoral, you make me feel as if—

THE DOVE: As if?

VERA: Well, as if your terrible quality were not one of action, but just the opposite, as if you wanted to prevent nothing.

THE DOVE: There are enough people preventing things, aren't there?

VERA: Yes—that's why you frighten me.

THE DOVE: Because I let everything go on, as far as it can go?

VERA: Yes, because you disturb nothing.

THE DOVE: I see.

VERA: You never meddle—

THE DOVE: No, I never meddle.

VERA: You don't even observe as other people do, you don't watch. Why, if I were to come to you, wringing my hands saying, "Amelia has shot herself," I don't believe you would stand up.

154

THE DOVE: No, I don't suppose I would, but I would do something for all that.

VERA: What?

THE DOVE: I should want to be very sure you wrung your hands as much as possible, and that Amelia had gotten all there was to get out of the bullet before she died.

VERA: It's all very well, but why don't you do something?

THE DOVE: A person who is capable of anything needs no practice.

VERA: You are probably maligning yourself, you are a gentle creature, a very girl—

THE DOVE: If you were sensitive you would not say that.

VERA: Well, perhaps. [*She laughs a hard laugh.*] What can you expect of a lumber dealer's daughter?

THE DOVE: Why are you so restless, Vera?

VERA: Because I'm a woman. I leave my life entirely to my imagination and my imagination is terrific. I can't even turn to religion, for the *prie-dieu* inclines me to one thing only—so there you are!

THE DOVE: You imagine—many things?

VERA: You know well enough—sitting here day after day, giving my mind everything to do, the body nothing—

THE DOVE: What do you want, Vera?

VERA: Some people would say a lover, but I don't say a lover; some people would say a home, but I don't say a home. You see I have imagined myself beyond the need of the usual home and beyond the reach of the usual lover—

THE DOVE: Then?

VERA: Perhaps what I really want is a reason for using one of these pistols! [*She laughs and lies back.* THE

DOVE, *having risen, goes up behind* VERA *and places her hand on her throat.*]

THE DOVE: Now you may use one of those pistols.

VERA: [*startled, but making no attempt to remove* THE DOVE'S *hand.*] For such a *little* thing?

THE DOVE: [*dropping her hand, once more taking up her old position, sword on knee*] Ah!

VERA: Why do you say that? [*She is evidently agitated.*]

THE DOVE: I suppose I shall *always* wait.

VERA: What is the matter?

THE DOVE: Always, always!

VERA: What is the matter?

THE DOVE: I suppose I'm waiting for the person who will know that anything is a reason for using a pistol, unless one is waiting for the obvious, and the obvious has never been sufficient reason.

VERA: It's all hopeless, I am hopeless and Amelia is hopeless, and as for you— [*She makes a gesture.*]

THE DOVE: I've never held anything against hopelessness.

VERA: Now what do you mean?

THE DOVE: It doesn't matter.

VERA: [*after a long pause*] I wish you danced.

THE DOVE: Perhaps I do.

VERA: It might make me happier.

THE DOVE: [*irrelevantly*] Why don't people get angry at each other, quite suddenly and without reason?

VERA: Why should they?

THE DOVE: Isn't there something fine and cold and detached about a causeless anger?

VERA: I suppose so, it depends

THE DOVE: No, it does not depend, that's exactly it; to have a reason is to cheapen rage. I wish every man were beyond the reach of his own biography.

VERA: You are either quite an idiot, or a saint.

THE DOVE: I thought we had discussed that.

VERA: [*dashed but not showing it*] Yes, a saint.

THE DOVE: [*continuing*] I'm impatient of necessary continuity, I'm too sensitive, perhaps. I want the beautiful thing to be, how can logic have anything to do with it, or probable sequence?

VERA: You make my hair stand on end!

THE DOVE: Of course, that's logical!

VERA: Then how is it you like Amelia? And how do you stand me?

THE DOVE: Because you are two splendid dams erected about two little puddles.

VERA: You're horrid!

THE DOVE: Only horrid!

VERA: Yes, I'm really afraid of you.

THE DOVE: Afraid?

VERA: For instance, when you're out of this room all these weapons might be a lot of butter knives or pop guns, but let you come in—

THE DOVE: Well?

VERA: It becomes an arsenal.

THE DOVE: Yet you call me the Dove.

VERA: Amelia called you the Dove, I'd never have thought of it. It's just like Amelia to call the only dangerous thing she ever knew the "Dove."

THE DOVE: Yes, there's something in that.

VERA: Shall I sing for you?

THE DOVE: If you like.

VERA: Or shall I show you the album that no one ever sees? [*She laughs.*] If we had any friends we would have to throw that book in the fire.

THE DOVE: And you would have to clear the entry—

VERA: True. It's because of that picture of the Venetian courtesans that I send Amelia out for the butter, I don't dare let the grocer call.

THE DOVE: You have cut yourselves off—just because you're lonely.

VERA: Yes, just because we are lonely.

THE DOVE: It's quite wonderful.

VERA: It's a wonder the neighbors don't complain of Amelia's playing that way on the violin.

THE DOVE: I had not noticed.

VERA: No, I presume not, but every one else in the house has. No nice woman slurs as many notes as Amelia does! [*At this moment* AMELIA *enters the outer room. She is wearing a cloak with three shoulder-capes, a large plumed hat, and skirt with many flounces.*]

AMELIA: [*from the entry*] You should come and see Carpaccio's Deux Courtisanes Vénitiennes now, the sun is shining right in on the head of the one in the foreground. [*She begins to hum an Italian street song.*] Well, I have brought a little something and a bottle of wine. The wine is for you, my Dove—and for you, Vera, I've a long green feather. [*Pause in which* THE DOVE *continues to polish the blade of the sword.* VERA *has picked up her book.*]

AMELIA: [*advancing into the room, shrugging*] It's damp! [*seeing* THE DOVE *still at work*] What a sweet, gentle creature, what a little Dove it is! Ah, God, it's a sin, truly it's a sin that I, a woman with temperament, permit a young girl to stay in the same room with me!

THE DOVE: [*in a peaceful voice*] I've loaded all the pistols—

VERA: [*with suppressed anger*] Shined all the swords, ground all the poniard points! Attack a man now if you dare, he'll think you're playing with him!

AMELIA: [*in an awful voice*] Vera! [*She begins pacing.*] Disaster! disaster!—wherever I go, disaster! A woman selling fish tried to do me out of a quarter and when I remonstrated with her, she said with a wink: "I, too, have been bitten by the fox!"

THE DOVE: If you'll sit down I'll make some tea.

AMELIA: No, no, we'll have a little lunch soon, only I never can get the corks out of bottles.

THE DOVE: I can.

VERA: Rubbish! [*She gets up and goes out.*]

AMELIA: Well, has anything happened since I went out?

THE DOVE: No.

AMELIA: No, no, it never does. [*She begins to walk about hurriedly.*] Aren't there a great many flies in here?

THE DOVE: Yes, the screens should be put up.

AMELIA: No, no, no, I don't want anything to be shut out. Flies have a right to more than life, they have a right to be curious.

THE DOVE: A bat flew into the room last night.

AMELIA: [*shuddering*] Some day I shall look like a bat, having beaten my wings about every corner of the world, and never having hung over anything but myself—

THE DOVE: And this morning, early, before you got up, the little seamstress' monkey walked in through the window—

AMELIA: [*stopping short*] Are we to become infested?

THE DOVE: Yesterday the mailman offered me some dancing mice, he's raising them.

AMELIA: [*throwing up her hands*] There! You see! [*pause*] Why should I wear red heels? Why does my heart beat?

THE DOVE: Red heels are handsome.

AMELIA: Yes, yes, that's what I say. [*She begins to dance.*] Little one, were you ever held in the arms of the one you love?

THE DOVE: Who knows?

AMELIA: If we had not been left an income we might have been in danger—well, let us laugh. [*She takes a few more dance steps.*] Eating makes one fat, nothing more, and exercising reduces one, nothing more. Drink wine—put flesh on the instep, the instep that used to tell such a sweet story—and then the knees—fit for nothing but prayers! The hands—too fat to wander! [*She waves her arm.*] Then one exercises, but it's never the same; what one has, is always better than what one regains. Is it not so, my little one? But never mind, don't answer. I'm in an excellent humor—I could talk for hours, all about myself—to myself, for myself. God! I'd like to tear out all the wires in the house! Destroy all the tunnels in the city, leave nothing underground or hidden or useful, oh, God, God! [*She has danced until she comes directly in front of* THE DOVE. *She drops on her knees and lays her arms on either side of*

THE DOVE.] I hate the chimneys on the houses, I hate the doorways, I hate you, I hate Vera, but most of all I hate my red heels!

THE DOVE: [*almost inaudibly*] Now, now!

AMELIA: [*in high excitement*] Give me the sword! It has been sharpened long enough, give it to me, give it to me ! [*She makes a blind effort to find the sword; finding* THE DOVE'S *hand instead, she clutches it convulsively. Slowly* THE DOVE *bares Amelia's left shoulder and breast, and leaning down, sets her teeth in. Amelia gives a slight, short, stifled cry. At the same moment* VERA *appears in the doorway with the uncorked bottle.* THE DOVE *stands up swiftly, holding a pistol. She turns in the doorway hastily vacated by* VERA.]

THE DOVE: So! [*She bows, a deep military bow, and turning goes into the entry.*]

THE VOICE OF THE DOVE: For the house of Burgson! [*A moment later a shot is heard.*]

AMELIA: [*running after her*] Oh, my God!

VERA: What has she done?

AMELIA: [*reappearing in the doorway with the picture of the Venetian courtesans, through which there is a bullet hole—slowly, but with emphasis*] *This* is obscene!

[*curtain*]

WATER-ICE

Wherein the Wintry Lady Fiora Silvertree
is Unexpectedly Thawed

Vanity Fair, XX (July 1923)

The curtain is up, disclosing a room entirely cool and entirely white.

The room is large and almost untouched by color. White, in many materials; deep haired polar rugs; chairs in thick embroidered satin; walls of lacquer; candelabrum of twisted crystal; porcelains, misshapen like dead flowers; a bowl of shaved ice, exhaling a cool steam. In clear basins, thin depths of white Assyrian rose waters lie. The fire burns clear; the logs are of white pine.

About a goblet, spilling a thick cluster of lemon-pale grapes, lie masses of gardenias.

Upon a couch of dull cloth, a fan of cocque, as crisp as chalk, has been tossed.

The double windows look out upon trees sharp with ice. The curtains at these windows are so thick that they might have been lifted from a pan of milk on a dairy-maid's thumb.

By these curtains, in draperies somber and lusterless, paces LADY FIORA SILVERTREE. *She is austere, beautiful and passionless; she is thin beyond necessity. Her sockets, moving, touch off light where her knee bends in her gown. Her cheek bones are ivory beneath a faultless skin. Her light eyes are shadowed by many days of seclusion. In her ears tremble crystal drops, and her fingers are burdened to the knuckles with diamonds; in her hair quivers a Chinese flower of white jade.*

As she walks, her hands are clasped behind her; impassive she is, and undisturbed. In her gaze there is neither interest nor the lack of it; a still, locked existence.

Beside her, in precise lengths, a Russian wolfhound paces, with the curve of a sickle.

It may be noted that the mouth of LADY FIORA SILVERTREE *passes out of the realm of colorless things, to return to them again in the curve of a close underlip.*

Presently a maid enters, spotless in linens. She arranges a chair, facing the audience. She places a white cushion at its foot, and a crystal ashtray before it. She prepares to draw the curtains.

LADY FIORA: What hour is it, Lily?

LILY: It is three minutes to four o'clock, Madame.

LADY FIORA: Bring, presently, two glasses of lime-juice, sweetened with rock-candy and diluted with spring water. Bring also the incense that does not smoke.

LILY: Yes, madame. [*She leaves the room, returning with a censor. In a few moments she announces* MAJOR OTTOMAN, *a tall man in the white liveries of a high military order in the country of Avalon.*]

OTTOMAN: [*bowing deeply*] Madame.

LADY FIORA: Please sit down: for the time being I will stand.

OTTOMAN: [*seating himself, uncomfortably*] Today is the

last day of the year—I have been commanded to present myself to you, Madame, in order—

LADY FIORA: Exactly, they were my orders, but before you continue, I wish to acquaint you with the real gravity of the situation. [LILY *enters, with two crystal goblets of lime-juice and water. Placing them on a small table, she leaves the room.*] I am Lady Fiora Silvertree, the most beautiful and coldest woman in Avalon. Once, I was followed on the streets by multitudes. All the men of Avalon pursued me, old men, young men. They hung upon my every word. Men named their children for me; for me was the festival of flowers. That was ten years ago. I, sir, gave up the life of passion and emotion ten years ago today, knowing how base, how shallow man is and how his word goes for naught, and how lies alone make progress from mouth to mouth, and that there is wisdom in no one. I came here and I had the doors locked and the windows screened by eighty yards of stuffed silk, that I might not behold the false seasons pass and go. Winter alone is to my liking, and for her alone I permit my curtains to be drawn. It is now the time of ice. White ice pleases me.

I chose this cloistered abode, which is like the virgin mind of a child of no hours, thoughtless and unprejudiced and blank, and here I walk the year away, seeing no one but my maid and speaking to no one save her; she answering only when I command her so to do. Here, one day, away from the senseless devotion of men and of the city, I, Fiora Silvertree, shall die, please God, and ascend to heaven, without a last word, without a philosophy. Neither shall I be burdened with a fanatical love for another, I shall ascend simply, as a featherless arrow, intent upon no target.

OTTOMAN: [*leaning forward*] And madame has never known what it was to love a man, the frenzied pursuit of love?

LADY FIORA: [*coldly, lowering her thin lids*] You are impudent, sir, no one is permitted to question me. Nevertheless, this once, because I have never seen you before and never shall again, I will answer you. I loved a man once. His name was Lucien: he and I loved as no others in the world have ever loved before. I reverenced his love, but I had firmly resolved to remain celibate. Then I came here, and here I have remained.

OTTOMAN: And once, every year—

LADY FIORA: [*interrupting*] Once, every year, on that year's last day, a messenger comes to me from the outer world, to tell me one thing, and one thing only; the most important tidings for the past twelve months in Avalon. This, then, I would know of you.

OTTOMAN: And what have the nine other messages been, madame?

LADY FIORA: [*wearily, and touching with chill fingertips the pearls of her close corsage*] For ten years there has been nothing but repetition. No one has brought me tidings of anything save that which I knew full well. No happening worthy to pierce a virgin's ear that has known silence for three hundred and sixty-four days. Nine different messengers have come, as you have come today, and each, unknown to the other, has brought the same message, couched in the same terms: "The men of Avalon cry out for Fiora's beauty. And one—heartbrokened, bereft—who goes by the name of Lucien, stands before the Virgin in the cathedral crying softly into the stuff of his sleeve, vowing eternal love to Lady Fiora."

OTTOMAN: [*sipping the iced lime*] It is indeed an insult to a recluse of celibate mind.

LADY FIORA: You are the first of my messengers who has been allowed to speak so many words beside the point.

OTTOMAN: Madame, I am humbled. [*offering her a cigarette*] Will you?

LADY FIORA: I never smoke.

OTTOMAN: Why?

LADY FIORA: You have too many questions. Still I will answer you. Know then that I do not smoke because it turns the white of the eye a saffron color, not to my liking.

OTTOMAN: [*lighting his cigarette*] May I?

LADY FIORA: Certainly. And now perhaps it were well you should tell me of the great events that have come to pass in Avalon for the twelve-month past.

OTTOMAN: [*rising and bowing*] As you will madame, and this time I think I have news that will please you. [*He speaks in a tone quite devoid of interest.*] This thing was not so until the trees hardened and the ground thickened and the time of snow was upon us. But now it is. The men of Avalon no longer speak of you. They have ceased mourning your lost beauty; and Lucien has quite forgotten you.

LADY FIORA: [*her hand is at her throat; her pale eyes darkening, the red of her lips a most dangerous scar-*

let] I thank you. [*They bow, and* OTTOMAN *passes out silently. For a moment she is alone. She does not move. She seems not to take breaths, then, furiously, like one gone mad, she begins to tear off her earrings, her pearls, and to loosen the locks of her hair. She overturns the goblet of white grapes. She commands her Russian wolfhound to cease his pacing, and hangs upon the bell-cord until* LILY *enters, clasping her hands.*] Quick, quick!

LILY: Madame, madame. What is it?

LADY FIORA: Fool, have you no blood in you; no heat? Bring me my scarlet dress, my golden slippers, and my mantle of lavender brocade.

LILY: [*wringing her hands*] Oh! madame, madame what will you do?

LADY FIORA: Walk in the streets again, little goose; seek Lucien—and warmer weather; there is too much white ice in my spine. [*She begins to unfasten her bodice.*]

[*curtain*]

THE BEAUTY

Shadowland, IX (October 1923)

The boudoir of KATRINA MALEVOLITCH. *It is spacious and luxurious, inflamed by highly colored cushions and dangerous-looking icons, in front of which burn candles with steady red flames. A jeweled samovar stands beside a couch. A smoking cigarette butt in an ashtray at the foot of this couch, proclaims the recent presence of the mistress. At the moment, however, no one but* PRINCE IVAN VOLOVAIN *is in the room. He is strapped into as many military garments as possible, and he walks up and down rapidly, dragging a sword behind him. As he walks he twirls, with sensitive and nervous fingers, a moustache no less sensitive and nervous.*

He has kissed each of the icons three or four times, crossing and uncrossing himself. The curtains part with a swish of fury as the handsome KATRINA MALEVOLITCH *bounds into the room.*

KATRINA: [*with bright boredom*] Ah, my beautiful, rough Russian!

IVAN: Katrina, do not trifle with me. The season dies, the snows do not melt from my dooryard. I cross myself before the icons and say: "Is it true, Ivan Volovain, that you suffer so?" And women come and women go, but none are as beautiful as you.

KATRINA: [*twisting her many rings about on her many fingers*] I've heard all that before, Ivan. Tell me something new. [*She seats herself, rolling a cigarette.*] We women are all tired of the old custom. The siege must clothe itself in new garments.

IVAN: What can a man in love say? You are the passion of my life. I can no longer command. My rank will be taken from me. Your face, your carriage, your beauty—

KATRINA: [*breaking the cigarette in two*] There! My beauty once more! Are women never to be loved for anything else?

IVAN: But, madame—

KATRINA: [*raising her dark, flashing eyes*] Ivan Volovain, for three years I have suffered your attentions. I have heard you repeat the same phrases over and over, until my soul dies. I have allowed myself to be degraded by the spectacle of a man who calls admiration for a pretty face love. I am tired of love. I am tired of this beauty. I will hear no more of it! The man I marry must think me as ugly as a rusty sledge, and as mental as a medical dictionary. He must take me as an equal, or—or—[*She breaks down, weeping bitterly into a pocket handkerchief.*] Or I'll remain as I am, always—always—That's my answer, and don't let me see you again ever—ever—

   He stands wringing his hands for a moment, blushes deeply, bows, kisses the icons all over again, pours himself a glass of tea, drinks it, and goes out without a backward glance.

KATRINA: [*ringing for the maid*] Show in such suitors as

may have collected in my reception room; refill the samovar, and don't disturb me.

KATRINA *drapes herself appropriately, draws a concertina to her, lies back inhaling the black smoke of a wicked-looking cheroot. Enter, on kitten feet, the clerk* POPOVIM. *He has watering blue eyes and a feeble blond moustache. His timidity makes his hair stand along his brow in a ridge of terror.*

POPOVIM: Princess—

KATRINA: [*not looking up*] Ah, you. Well, Popovim, what can I do for you? You suffer, you cannot sleep, the snow falls, and you are not satisfied with nature—

POPOVIM: No, Princess, I—

KATRINA: [*waving to the samovar*] Take a sip of tea, it will strengthen you—

POPOVIM: [*timidly approaching the samovar, dropping a glove in his confusion*] No, Princess, I thank you, but—

KATRINA: [*angrily, springing to her elbow*] Are you in love with me, or aren't you? You ridiculous fellow!

POPOVIM: [*in abject confusion*] No, Princess, no, not at all—

KATRINA: [*slowly*] What?

POPOVIM: Not at all. That is, certainly. Anything you like. Your humble servant, to walk on, to deride, to analyze to your heart's content, but—

KATRINA: [*annoyed*] But *what?*

POPOVIM: My children, madame—

KATRINA: This goes too far! [*ringing*] Send in another man, this one is a father.

POPOVIM *is hustled off with the help of his collar, while he tries to stop his trembling and to explain his visit. A stout man, bald and wearing a great-beaked nose with some satisfaction, enters. He is carrying a bundle.*

KATRINA: [*lying back*] And what is your name?

HE: [*bowing*] Smerdkin, your highness—

KATRINA: Well, Smerdkin?

SMERDKIN: [*dropping his parcel which he manages to recover*] I am honored, Princess, it is good of you to see me. For seven years I have tried to gain access to your presence. Now at last the stars are with me. The Great Bear and the Little Bear were seen embracing in the sky last Tuesday week—

KATRINA: Nonsense. I am bored. [*She rolls another cigarette.*] Well?

SMERDKIN: I have here—

KATRINA: [*suppressing a yawn*] Presents, presents! Last year a suitor gave me a miniature ice palace standing five inches high, with minarets and a bell in it that tinkled if one pushed it with one's finger, so—well?

SMERDKIN: No, madame, I have here something even more deserving of your attention—

KATRINA: [*with little interest*] Well, what is it? I am tired of gifts, you know.

SMERDKIN: Then you have in store a great happiness, Princess. [*He has managed to untie the parcel and a length of narrow fur falls to the floor and rolls away under the couch.*]

KATRINA: Great heavens! What is that?

SMERDKIN: The house of Smerdkin and Smerdoff sent

me out seven years ago, with this sample of weavel skin to show to your highness. It is intended as insertion for all delicate things. The handkerchief, the dressing-robe, as trimmings for ashtrays, for earrings—

KATRINA: [*livid with fury*] Wretch, how dare you! Disturbing me this early in the day to try to make an odious sale! You should be stabbed in the back!

KATRINA *rings, and* SMERDKIN *is shown out hurriedly, somewhat in the manner of* POPOVIM. *In a moment a tall man, wearing spectacles and carrying a strapped bundle of books comes into the room. He coughs, but it is a defiant cough, made audible not to get her attention, but simply to display itself for its own egotistic ends.*

HE: Katrina Malevolitch, I believe?

KATRINA: [*preening herself in all her handsome length*] Quite. And you.

FYODOR GONGEROV: Gongerov—student.

KATRINA: Of?

GONGEROV: Botany and auto-intoxication.

KATRINA: How cute!

GONGEROV: Let us get to the point. [*Without waiting to be invited to sit, he does so, laying the bundle of books across his knees.*] I hear that you are a wealthy woman. I am a man of small means. I have a great work to perform for the Russian people. I am trying to put flowers on an equal footing with vegetables. Without your help all my endeavors will be lost. As a woman you mean nothing at all to me. You may be dyspeptic, and cross-eyed. It makes no difference. You mean nothing to me physically, and you never will.

Therefore, being just, if I marry you, your time and your inclinations may run neck to neck. I shall be too occupied with my studies to notice—

KATRINA: [*slowly, rising on her elbow*] Do you mean that?

GONGEROV: Of course, I mean it. Your career is your own, and if you really have one I shall not be as ashamed of the marriage as I expect to be.

KATRINA: [*pale, her hand to her face*] Have you ever *seen* me before?

GONGEROV: Certainly, out driving with that fellow, an officer, I believe—and you are always the same.

KATRINA: [*coy*] And how is that?

GONGEROV: Just a few yards of white and pink flesh, wound about an inadequate skeleton.

At this moment IVAN *puts his head through the curtains behind* GONGEROV, *unseen by the student, but quite visible to* KATRINA.

KATRINA: [*regaining poise*] Continue.

GONGEROV: In this book there is the most poignant description of the failings of women. They are high-hipped and lazy, they encumber themselves with clothes; they simper, whine and are willful. They tear a man down from the high position in which God placed him.

At this precise moment IVAN *collars him, jerks him off his chair, tosses him lightly in the snow without, and takes up his wooing where he left off.*

IVAN: I cross myself and I say: "Is it possible, Ivan Volovain, that you suffer so?" The sleigh bells only exceed the sleighs coming and going, and women from here to Moscow turn to the arms of their lovers. I, I alone, live solitary and desolate in this country that has but one Katrina, and but one beauty.

KATRINA: [*lying back, lighting another cheroot*] Our psychologies are almost too rich for this world, are they not, Ivan?

IVAN: Absolutely.

KATRINA: We must be careful. I am brain-weary. You may kiss me.

SHE TELLS HER DAUGHTER

Smart Set, LXXII (November 1923)

The interior of a handsomely decorated drawing room. It is paneled in brocaded heron-blue satin. Twisted glass and candlesticks throw a shower of sparks into the cool surfaces of many mirrors.

The studied odor of tiger lilies pervades the air, mixed with the sweet, faint perfume of a single flower used in the talcum affected by ELLEN LOUISE THERESA DEERFONT, *and through them both, like a sharp and pointed arrow, the piercing arrangement of some oriental bouquet exhaled from the every movement of* MADAME DEERFONT.

MADAME DEERFONT *stands by a slender Italian chair. She is pretending to read the pages of a smart French journal.*

ELLEN LOUISE THERESA *is perusing, with a nefariously Greek nose, the pages of* The Book of Beautiful Women, *shaking, from time to time, a globular curl over thin, languid shoulders. She is obviously sixteen.*

MADAME DEERFONT: My dear, you have reached maturity. It is time that I should talk to you seriously.

ELLEN LOUISE THERESA: But I know all about it, mother.

MADAME DEERFONT: I don't know what you mean

when you say you know all about it, but what I am going to tell you, you can't possibly know; the true story of my life.

ELLEN LOUISE THERESA: [*settling herself comfortably*] Oh, I know all that. You were born in England, you fell in love with a fellow named Percy, you went to school, you met papa—

MADAME DEERFONT: [*nervously fingering the stopper of the pot-pourri*] No, that is not it. There must be a bond of fundamentals between us from now on. I want you to know me, not as I appear to the audience or those who accept the hospitality of my home, but as I am, dark, obscure, terrible—

ELLEN LOUISE THERESA: Mother, do behave! What is so dreadful in the fact that you are an actress and smoke cigarettes?

MADAME DEERFONT: [*crumbling leaves between her jewelled fingers*] What a child you are, so young, so inexperienced—

ELLEN LOUISE THERESA: I'm not. I just don't see any reason for taking all this so tragically.

MADAME DEERFONT: That is the very attitude of youth, Ellen Louise Theresa. Let us begin at the beginning. I was the daughter of a chemist.

ELLEN LOUISE THERESA: [*startled*] Why, I thought—

MADAME DEERFONT: Exactly, you thought I was the daughter of an M.P. Well this is the first blow, but the truth is the truth.

I was born in Brooklyn; I never saw England. I was improperly educated. I was waspish. I used to torment animals—

ELLEN LOUISE THERESA: [*excited*] O-Oh, did you kill cats?

MADAME DEERFONT: [*visibly agitated*] I am not going into details. Then when I was fourteen I met Ramey in a cigarette shop—

ELLEN LOUISE THERESA: Why, mother, did you smoke at that age?

MADAME DEERFONT: [*evasively*] They were for your grandfather. Well, anyway I met Ramey. He was consumptive. He had nervous ways with his hands. I was very sorry for him, and excited because I thought he was dying...slowly—

ELLEN LOUISE THERESA: Why, mother—

MADAME DEERFONT: He was very grateful to me. I took him up into the garret and we read *Hamlet* together, and he recited bits of the "Lily Maid," and he looked so pitiful, and yet so touching that...[*aside*] I can't go into that; she would never understand. [*aloud*]—then he went away—

ELLEN LOUISE THERESA: Didn't you ever kiss him?

MADAME DEERFONT: [*vaguely*] I don't remember.

ELLEN LOUISE THERESA: [*now thoroughly interested*] Go on!

MADAME DEERFONT: *I* was morose for a time, until I was about eighteen, then a thing happened—[*She breaks off; a shower of leaves falls back into the jar.*] I have always been thoughtful by temperament; I had been left too much alone. Perhaps my mother was to blame. She was always crying and making my father nervous and drawing our heads down onto her bosom saying, "I shall never recover," and of course no one ever recovers from the mortal blow of life, and eventually she died. She could not let up even then. Dying, she said to my father, rising up on her elbow, her lace falling away in a wild and disordered cascade, "You see, I told you so." Then I was alone a year with my father, thinking about it all the time. One day a man came into the shop, asking for some medicine. He was thin and not particularly good looking, but there was something passionate in that look—terrible and excessive. I watched him from the crack of the door. I remember what I thought. I said to myself: "He has believed something I do not know or understand." He went away presently. I came out and talked to my father. He let me paste labels on bottles. I wanted to put on only those marked Poison, but he said that was ridiculous, and he would not let me—finally he came back one day, while I was singing—

ELLEN LOUISE THERESA: Who?

MADAME DEERFONT: The same young man.

ELLEN LOUISE THERESA: What were you singing?

MADAME DEERFONT: I don't remember. I think it was "In My Lady's Chamber." Well, he stepped right into the room and took my hands off the keys and he said in a peculiarly quiet voice: "Now, that's enough of that."

ELLEN LOUISE THERESA: How funny!

MADAME DEERFONT: [*hysterically, putting her black lace handkerchief to her mouth*] Yes, wasn't it. So we got to be very good friends—only—

ELLEN LOUISE THERESA: Only what?

MADAME DEERFONT: My father forbade me to see him, because of the way he walked directly into the room, taking my hands off the keys. Father saw that and was angry—but we met—often—mostly at night.

ELLEN LOUISE THERESA: Were the nights awfully dark?

MADAME DEERFONT: Yes, quite dark. I used to get out of bed, put my slippers and dressing gown on, and tip-toe down the stairs—my room was at the head of the back stairs—and my heart beat so—

ELLEN LOUISE THERESA: [*excited*] So what?

MADAME DEERFONT: The locket on my neck trembled. We would hide in the corner of the garden, or go to his place. His father kept a livery stable. We would crawl into the hay and laugh and were frightened—

ELLEN LOUISE THERESA: [*with conviction*] My, you were a bad girl!

MADAME DEERFONT: [*quickly*] We could smell the varnishes on the different carriages. "That is red," I would say, he would answer, "No, that's a black varnish smell." Sometimes, if we did not know what to say, he would show me the harnesses, places where they had been mended with round copper nails; the saddles, the combs and brushes. I liked tasting the lump salt where the tongues of the horses had worn it smooth and shiny, and I felt eager and amazed.

ELLEN LOUISE THERESA: Why?

MADAME DEERFONT: [*becoming more and more agitated*] Then one night he told me he loved me, and after that—everything seemed nearer to me. I could not bear the summer nights because they were so all about me, and the stars in the sky seemed to be so terribly far away, but yet they seemed to be at a distance from *me*—but you can't understand all that. After several months he went away.

ELLEN LOUISE THERESA: Don't skip parts like that.

MADAME DEERFONT: I did not look at the sky. Sometimes I went to the barn and lay in the hay, thinking—

ELLEN LOUISE THERESA: What about? Didn't you like him anymore?

MADAME DEERFONT: I thought about danger and— death. [*aside*] It's no use—

ELLEN LOUISE THERESA: Why don't you go on, now you've got to the most exciting part?

MADAME DEERFONT: One night while I was lying in the hay, he came in. I could hear him breathing among the horses. I remember his breathing because it was so hurried among that big, slow breathing all about, and I sat up holding the knife so hard that the handle cut into my flesh—

ELLEN LOUISE THERESA: Knife! What knife?

MADAME DEERFONT: Oh, a knife I found lying in the hay, his, an English blade that set into the handle when not in use, but when it was, it would not bend, or shut, or be safe. When he got near I— [*She is so agitated that she cannot continue.*]

ELLEN LOUISE THERESA: [*childishly, clapping her hands*] It's so exciting! Then what did you do?

MADAME DEERFONT: [*aside*] I can't tell her. [*aloud*] Then? Why nothing. I went away, quietly—home—

ELLEN LOUISE THERESA: Didn't you ever see him again?

MADAME DEERFONT: No, I never saw him again, but lots of people went to the funeral—

ELLEN LOUISE THERESA: Funeral! What funeral? Did he die?

MADAME DEERFONT: [*laughing, high-pitched*] How silly of me to forget the point of the story! Of course he died. He killed himself.

ELLEN LOUISE THERESA: [*wide-eyed*] Oh! How?

MADAME DEERFONT: Why with that knife, right in his shirt, over the heart, he must have died instantly— without a regret, as they say— [*The stopper of the jar snaps in her fingers.*]

ELLEN LOUISE THERESA: And is that all?

MADAME DEERFONT: That's all. Your father married me then, he was always good, you must remember that. He said he would help me out of my trouble, and he did.

ELLEN LOUISE THERESA: What trouble?

MADAME DEERFONT: Why my father, he had made things very uncomfortable for me. He had married again, a great lazy brute of a creature called Daisy, I could not bear it. I wanted a home of my own.

ELLEN LOUISE THERESA: Then you came here?

MADAME DEERFONT: Heavens no! We had a little apartment for a while overlooking the bay. Then shortly you were born. You must always love and respect your father.

ELLEN LOUISE THERESA: Why, of course—

MADAME DEERFONT: [*aside*] It's the best I could do, she would not have understood. [*aloud*] Then after that, perhaps three or so more years, we came here, and here we have lived, happily ever after.

ELLEN LOUISE THERESA: [*disentangling herself from the chair, in a blasé voice*] Well you see, I did know all about it, all but a few details; Brooklyn, and all that sort of thing.

MADAME DEERFONT: [*lighting a cigarette*] Yes, of course, all but a few details.

[*curtain*]

DJUNA BARNES

Long seen as a legendary figure by her admirers, Djuna Barnes has increasingly come to be recognized over the past few decades as a major American author. She is best known for her fictional masterwork, *Nightwood,* an anatomy; but she also wrote other works of fiction, *A Book* (reprinted as *A Night Among the Horses* and later, with new stories and substantial revisions, as *Spillway*) and *Ryder.* She also published an almanac, *Ladies Almanack,* and a drama, *The Antiphon.* Sun & Moon Press has published a selection of her early stories as *Smoke and Other Early Stories,* selected her theatrical interviews in *Interviews,* and brought together several of her writings on New York City in *New York.* Other plays planned are *Biography of Julie von Bartmann; Ann Portuguise;* and a new edition of *The Antiphon.*

With Eugene O'Neill and Edna St. Vincent Millay, Barnes was an early member of the Provincetown Players. Later, in the 1920s, she lived in Paris, where her wit and brilliant writing won her close friendships with T.S. Eliot, James Joyce, Peggy Guggenheim, and other well-known American expatriates. When she returned to the United States, she wrote for *The Theater Guild Magazine.* She died in New York in 1982.

SUN & MOON CLASSICS

This publication was made possible, in part, through an operational grant from the Andrew W. Mellon Foundation and through contributions from the following individuals and organizations:

Tom Ahern (Foster, Rhode Island)
Charles Altieri (Seattle, Washington)
John Arden (Galway, Ireland)
Paul Auster (Brooklyn, New York)
Jesse Huntley Ausubel (New York, New York)
Luigi Ballerini (Los Angeles, California)
Dennis Barone (West Hartford, Connecticut)
Jonathan Baumbach (Brooklyn, New York)
Roberto Bedoya (Los Angeles, California)
Guy Bennett (Los Angeles, California)
Bill Berkson (Bolinas, California)
Steve Benson (Berkeley, California)
Charles Bernstein and Susan Bee (New York, New York)
Dorothy Bilik (Silver Spring, Maryland)
Alain Bosquet (Paris, France)
In Memoriam: John Cage
In Memoriam: Camilo José Cela
Rosita Copioli (Rimini, Italy)
Bill Corbett (Boston, Massachusetts)
Robert Crosson (Los Angeles, California)
Tina Darragh and P. Inman (Greenbelt, Maryland)
Fielding Dawson (New York, New York)
Christopher Dewdney (Toronto, Canada)
Larry Deyah (New York, New York)
Arkadii Dragomoschenko (St. Petersburg, Russia)
George Economou (Norman, Oklahoma)
Richard Elman (Stony Brook, New York)
Kenward Elmslie (Calais, Vermont)
Elaine Equi and Jerome Sala (New York, New York)
Lawrence Ferlinghetti (San Francisco, California)
Richard Foreman (New York, New York)
Howard N. Fox (Los Angeles, California)
Jerry Fox (Aventura, Florida)
In Memoriam: Rose Fox
Melvyn Freilicher (San Diego, California)
Miro Gavran (Zagreb, Croatia)

Allen Ginsberg (New York, New York)
Peter Glassgold (Brooklyn, New York)
Barbara Guest (Berkeley, California)
Perla and Amiram V. Karney (Bel Air, California)
Václav Havel (Prague, The Czech Republic)
Lyn Hejinian (Berkeley, California)
Fanny Howe (La Jolla, California)
Harold Jaffe (San Diego, California)
Ira S. Jaffe (Albuquerque, New Mexico)
Ruth Prawer Jhabvala (New York, New York)
Pierre Joris (Albany, New York)
Alex Katz (New York, New York)
Pamela and Rowan Klein (Los Angeles, California)
Tom LaFarge (New York, New York)
Mary Jane Lafferty (Los Angeles, California)
Michael Lally (Santa Monica, California)
Norman Lavers (Jonesboro, Arkansas)
Jerome Lawrence (Malibu, California)
Stacey Levine (Seattle, Washington)
Herbert Lust (Greenwich, Connecticut)
Norman MacAffee (New York, New York)
Rosemary Macchiavelli (Washington, DC)
Jackson Mac Low (New York, New York)
In Memoriam: Mary McCarthy
Harry Mulisch (Amsterdam, The Netherlands)
Iris Murdoch (Oxford, England)
Martin Nakell (Los Angeles, California)
In Memoriam: bpNichol
Cees Nooteboom (Amsterdam, The Netherlands)
NORLA (Norwegian Literature Abroad) (Oslo, Norway)
Claes Oldenburg (New York, New York)
Toby Olson (Philadelphia, Pennsylvania)
Maggie O'Sullivan (Hebden Bridge, England)
Rochelle Owens (Norman, Oklahoma)
Bart Parker (Providence, Rhode Island)
Marjorie and Joseph Perloff (Pacific Palisades, California)
Dennis Phillips (Los Angeles, California)
Carl Rakosi (San Francisco, California)
Tom Raworth (Cambridge, England)
David Reed (New York, New York)
Ishmael Reed (Oakland, California)
Tom Roberdeau (Los Angeles, California)

SUN & MOON CLASSICS

Hauser, Marianne	*The Long and the Short: Selected Stories* 138 ($12.95)
	Me & My Mom 36 ($9.95)
	Prince Ishmael 4 ($11.95)
Hawkes, John	*The Owl* and *The Goose on the Grave* 67 ($12.95)
Hejinian, Lyn	*The Cell* 21 ($11.95)
	The Cold of Poetry 42 ($12.95)
	My Life 11 ($9.95)
	Writing Is an Aid to Memory 141 ($10.95)
Hocquard, Emmanuel	*The Cape of Good Hope* 139 ($10.95)
Hoel, Sigurd	*The Road to the World's End* 75 ($13.95)
Howe, Fanny	*Radical Love* 82 ($21.95, cloth)
	The Deep North 15 ($9.95)
	Saving History 27 ($12.95)
Howe, Susan	*The Europe of Trusts* 7 ($10.95)
Jackson, Laura (Riding)	*Lives of Wives* 71 ($12.95)
James, Henry	*What Maisie Knew* 80 ($12.95)
Jenkin, Len	*Careless Love* 54 ($9.95)
	Dark Ride and Other Plays 22 ($13.95)
Jensen, Wilhelm	*Gradiva* 38 ($13.95)
Jones, Jeffrey M.	*J.P. Morgan Saves the Nation* 157 ($9.95)
	Love Trouble 78 ($9.95)
Katz, Steve	*43 Fictions* 18 ($12.95)
La Farge, Tom	*Terror of Earth* 136 ($12.95)
Larbaud, Valery	*Childish Things* 19 ($13.95)
Lins, Osman	*Nine, Novena* 104 ($13.95)
Mac Low, Jackson	*Barnesbook* 127 ($10.95)
	From Pearl Harbor Day to FDR's Birthday 126 ($10.95)
	Pieces O' Six 17 ($11.95)
Marinetti, F. T.	*Let's Murder the Moonshine: Selected Writings* 12 ($12.95)
	The Untameables 28 ($11.95)
Mathews, Harry	*Selected Declarations of Dependence* 128 ($10.95)

AMERICAN THEATER IN LITERATURE (ATL)

Developed by The Contemporary Arts Educational Project, Inc., a non-profit corporation, and published through its Sun & Moon Press, the American Theater in Literature program was established to promote American theater as a literary form and to educate readers about contemporary and modern theater. The program publishes work of major American playwrights as well as younger, developing dramatists in various publishing programs of the Press, including the Sun & Moon Classics (collections of plays of international significance), and in collaboration with specific theater groups such as En Garde Arts, the Mark Taper Forum, Primary Stages, Soho Rep, and the Undermain Theatre.

BOOKS IN THIS PROGRAM

Len Jenkin *Dark Ride and Other Plays* ($13.95)
(Sun & Moon Classics: 22)

Robert Auletta *The Persians* ($9.95)
(A Mark Taper Forum Play)

Matthew Maguire *The Tower* ($8.95)

Kier Peters *The Confirmation* ($6.95)

Len Jenkin *Careless Love* ($9.95)
(A Soho Rep Play / Sun & Moon Classics: 54)

Mac Wellman *The Land Beyond the Forest: Dracula* AND *Swoop* ($12.95)

Mac Wellman *Two Plays: A Murder of Crows* AND
The Hyacinth Macaw ($11.95)
(A Primary Stages Play / Sun & Moon Classics: 62)

Jeffrey Jones *Love Trouble* ($10.95)
(An Undermain Theatre Play / Sun & Moon Classics: 84)

Jeffrey Jones and Jonathan Larson *J.P. Morgan Saves the Nation* ($9.95)
(An En Garde Arts Play / Sun & Moon Classic: 157)

David Greenspan *Son of an Engineer* ($8.95)

Matthew Maguire *Phaedra* ($9.95)
(A Creation Production Company / Home for Contemporary Theatre Book)